The Haunting of Peter Ashton

The Haunting of Peter Ashton

Roberta L. Smith

This book is a work of fiction. Names, characters, places, and incidents are a product of the author's imagination or are used fictitiously. Any resemblance to actual events, institutions, business establishments, or persons living or deceased, is purely coincidental.

The Haunting of Peter Ashton

Copyright © 2023 by Roberta L. Smith

ISBN: 9798385856589

All rights reserved.

No part of this book may be reproduced, stored in a retrieval system, or transmitted in any form or by any means, electronic, mechanical, photocopying, recording, or otherwise, without written permission of the author.

www.bertabooks.com
www.robertalsmith.com
www.nevermoreenterprises.com

Books by Roberta L. Smith

The Secret of Lucianne Dove

Chapel Playhouse

The Accordo

The Dreamer of Downing Street

Bouquet of Lies

Simone's Ghosts

Distorted

Distorted 2

A Year in the Life of a Civil War Soldier, the 1864 Diary of Frank Steinbaugh

Brinkley the Kind-hearted Ghost

The Haunting of Peter Ashton was inspired by the author's short story, *The Comeback*, which can be found in her anthology, *Distorted 2.*

Chapter 1

Archibald Bent answered his cell on the first ring: "Dahling. I heard rumors you were trying to wriggle out of my party. It's a special party. I've spent a fortune on it and cancelations will not be tolerated, you should know that."

He checked his image in the rectangular cheval floor mirror that had enchanted him from the moment he discovered it in his favorite antique shop. He listened to the caller's stuttering response for a full twenty seconds before he heard, "Okay. No problem. I'll be there with bells on."

"You'll be here in the costume I sent you." They hung up and Archibald smiled like the sly old fox he was. He'd never met a friend he didn't love to torture.

He turned sideways, still gazing in the mirror, stuck out his chest and sucked in his gut, patting it slightly. If only he were ten pounds lighter his costume would show off to perfection.

Still, it was going to be marvelous.

He moved to the California King where the costume lay and touched the fabric of the pants. It was one in the afternoon, too early to don the outfit, but just looking at the clothing he'd had custom-made coursed satisfaction through his veins. He would wear the taupe 1880s-style artist's smock as he greeted his guests, then remove it later to reveal a form-fitting Victorian black coat and vest cut low enough to expose a white linen button-up shirt with a high collar that would cradle his neck. A narrow silk tie would constrict the collar and be finished off with a limp bow.

Perfect.

Archibald's glee was short lived when a crash sounded downstairs. He let loose with a few choice curse words before he rushed out as quickly as his aging, hobbling, sixty-seven-year-old frame would allow, moving one careful step at a time to the first floor of his nineteenth-century Victorian. Whatever was broken had better be something that belonged to Marta's Party Service, or she would get an earful and a bill.

He entered the Great Room through the nearer of its two entrances. The large space had been created out of what had once been a good-sized parlor and fair-sized servant's quarters. The remodel had only required one wall to be removed, so the integrity of the architecture had not been compromised.

Archibald saw black china hors d'oeuvre plates that didn't belong to him smashed to pieces on the floor. They hadn't made it to the long table covered with a lacy black cloth patterned with skulls. Also on the table were ten wine glasses decorated with metal skeleton hands, a punch-bowl cauldron, and black wax candles of varying heights arranged in clusters. It pleased Archibald to see Marta chewing out a petite young woman, twenty years old, if that, for breaking her dishes. "And don't think it isn't coming out of your wages, niece or no niece. Now sweep it up and don't miss anything!"

"Why not use paper plates like a normal person?" the girl impudently asked.

"Yours is not to reason why," her aunt replied.

"But to do or die," added Archibald.

The girl threw him a sullen look as the boss lady started for the hall that would take her to the kitchen.

"A little harsh with the help there, Marta," Archibald called out, the crafty smile he always kept at the ready on his lips. In truth he would have said much worse if the plates had been his.

"You want to pay for it, Archibald?" They'd known each other for ages.

Archibald snorted.

"I didn't think so," she said. He watched her disappear through the doorway, then glanced at the young employee who was also staring after Marta.

"My aunt's a bitch. I'm only here because she begged." The girl looked at the broken pieces on the parquet floor. "Maybe I'll just leave and she can clean it up herself."

"Would that be wise?"

The girl shrugged. "I don't care." She eyed Archibald as he eyed her. "My aunt said you used to be somebody. Wrote a hit movie or something a long time ago. But now you're a has-been."

"Did she now? It's a good thing I happen to know she has the intelligence of a toad. And it's two hit movies. And if anyone's a has-been . . . Did you know her claim to fame was being one of the June Taylor dancers?"

"Who?"

"Exactly." It wasn't true. Marta would have to be a hundred years old, or nearly. But an insult was an insult and the truth never bothered Archibald. He smirked. "You'll find a broom in the broom closet off the kitchen."

"Remy," she said.

"Excuse me?"

"My name is Remy, if we're going to have a conversation." She wandered over to one of ten sheet-covered shapes spread about the room, this one near a three-windowed wall. The windows allowed for a view of a beautiful, flower-permeated garden.

In addition to the ten ghost-like figures spread about the room, there were four tarp-covered areas that had to be hiding something of note because they were much larger and in varying configurations. One was ten feet tall, still well under the height of the twelve-foot-high ceiling.

"What is all this? My aunt said you're throwing a Halloween party. It's the middle of May."

"Is it? I hadn't noticed."

"You have fancy columns. They look like real concrete but they aren't. And statue-y thingies. And candelabras stuck to the walls."

"Sconces," Archibald corrected.

"Whatever. It looks like a movie set with all this stuff. Like a dungeon or something."

"Museum," Archibald clarified.

"The windows and garden don't fit in though. You should cover that."

"Not to worry. The windows will serve their purpose," Archibald defended dryly.

"And where are the witches and spiders and skulls and scary mirrors and stuff? Your ghosts are just lame."

"You insolent girl. They aren't ghosts. They're exactly what they look like. Sheets covering . . ." His eyes narrowed. One of the white shapes stood further to the left than earlier in the morning. "Did you move that?"

Remy followed his line of sight. "I didn't move anything." She frowned. "But now that you mention it, that one did start out over there." She pointed then looked at Archibald with an exaggerated expression of fear. After about five seconds she shouted, "Boo!"

Archibald flinched. Remy laughed. "My aunt and I moved it when we brought in the table. It was in the way."

"Hmmm," he fumed. He limped over to the figure, knowing it was heavier than he could handle by himself. "Come," he instructed. Remy took her time but eventually joined him. Together they scooted it back to where it had been.

"You didn't really answer my question," Remy said.

"Because I haven't a mind to."

Archibald's cell rang. He dug the phone out of a pocket and answered. "Sweetheart!" He listened. "No. You may not bring a plus-one. My invitation was not only handwritten but personal and specific. You and you alone." He listened. "You'll find out who I invited during the reveal. That is, if you survive the evening." He roared out a menacing cackle, only stopping after he received an insult from the caller. "I most certainly am not being cheesy." He hung up.

"You are being cheesy," Remy concurred.

Archibald shrugged with a lazy look of indifference. "So what? It's my bash."

"Why can't Sweetheart bring a plus one? It's a party!"

"*My* party. With a specific purpose." He stared at Remy and her curiosity made him feel like sharing. "Nine guests plus me. You've no doubt heard of Agatha Christie's *And Then There Were None*, also known as *Ten Little Indians*."

"Not really."

"Perhaps *House on Haunted Hill* rings a bell?"

"Sorry."

Archibald shook his head. "I wonder why I waste my breath."

"I'm just kidding. Of course I know *House on Haunted Hill*. I think my boyfriend has a video game."

"Not a video game." He groaned. "This party is to be a hybrid between all that and *House of Wax*. Hmmm?" He cocked his head and raised a brow, challenging her to have heard of that horror masterpiece.

"Goose egg," she informed him happily.

"Fine. It doesn't matter. To put it more succinctly, I plan to scare the bejeebers out of nine friends who done me wrong, as Mae West might have said."

"Who?"

"And I will be in costume as Vincent Price, or more accurately, Professor Henry Jerrod from the movie *House of Wax*."

"Who?" Remy looked more confused than ever.

This time Archibald couldn't contain himself. He threw both hands in the air and rolled his eyes. The generation gap was *just* too great. "Go on. Sweep up your mess. This has-been has a message to video." The doorbell rang and he smiled. "Ah. Thank goodness."

Archibald limped his way to the foyer and ushered in a skinny, baby-faced young man with curls of wild sandy hair. He wore Bermuda shorts and a clever white t-shirt with the saying on the front: **Electronic Technician — because freakin' miracle worker isn't an official job title**. Archibald acknowledged him by name. "Jordan."

"You'll never believe where I found her," the young man said excitedly as he stepped inside and dropped a duffle bag on the black-and-white patterned tile floor.

"I don't care where you found the thing, just that you did."

"It was my nephew. He can't resist a skull. Or in this case a skeleton."

"Spare me the details."

"So I'll set ol' Bessie up . . ."

"Bessie? What is she? The remains of some weepy-eyed maid from a nineteen-forties melodrama?"

The young man chuckled. "Good one, Arch."

"Don't call me Arch."

They started for the Great Room with Jordan babbling on about how he would retest everything he'd already installed and set up Bessie. Then he continued with how inventive he'd been and what a genius he was. Archibald simply tuned him out. "You do realize," he told Jordan, "that when I flip the switch, I don't care what makes the light come on."

Jordan laughed. "Another zinger, Arch—ibald. Hey, I checked out your last post on your website. So funny. But you should read the comments. Most people like Double A."

"Most people are cretins."

"Nah. She was good. I saw her in concert once. I think I was twelve. That was before she went to prison, of course. My brother was forced to take me along with him and his friends. Anyway, read the comments. A lot of people think you're a douche, but some agree with you."

"The non-cretins."

They entered the Great Room and found Remy busy sweeping up the shards of broken china. Jordan's eyes lit up at the sight of the pretty girl. He nearly hurried over to help her but Archibald held him back.

"You have the script I wrote?" Archibald asked.

Jordan patted his shorts pocket.

"And the costume so you'll blend in."

Jordan lifted the duffle bag. "With Bessie. I'll put it on last minute."

"Then I'll leave you to it. Just tell her—" he nodded in Remy's direction "—to stay in the kitchen. What I mean is, don't let her watch you. The fun stuff is none of her business."

"Right-o, Arch." Jordan saluted.

Archibald sighed and trudged upstairs, mumbling that he either needed to move or install an elevator.

He settled into a comfy, ergonomic office chair in front of his desktop computer and stretched out his arms. For several seconds he wiggled his arthritic fingers as though he was the maestro of all maestros not only because that was exactly how he thought of himself, but also because it helped to make them limber. Finally, he pulled up his website, found his post with the video, and clicked on play. A smile formed on his lips and he giggled at the words of wisdom that spilled from his mouth. He was extremely pleased with his cleverness.

"So Double A, known as Andrea Amber way back when, wrote these soulless, sappy, downright trite verses in her mother's basement when she hit the top of the charts with her first tone-deaf-public bona fide hit. Lyrically-challenged, she tries to be meaningful, squeezing out pathetic poetry only a parent could love. Whoever discovered this lost labor of garbage should be shot. No, I take that back. Whoever decided to release it to the masses that apparently haven't a clue what is shyte and what is Shinola should be drawn and quartered. There's a reason this discograph was left to expire in someone's long-lost archive. It should never have been resurrected but instead left to rot in its electronic grave, just as the dearly departed mass murderer Double A molders in hers."

Archibald patted himself on the shoulder. "Now that diatribe is music to my ears." It was a bit ironic that his rant actually attacked himself because he'd been a fan until Double A committed murder. Even that might not have turned him against her, but it was only by happenstance that he wasn't in the club the night she decided to burn it down. He might have been one of her victims, and he wouldn't forgive her for that. So never mind that he didn't truly believe what he was saying. The hate was real.

A song from the recently-released album poured from the computer speakers as Archibald lent his attention to the comments. There were those who loved his killer instinct, but many, many more were appalled.

Tone-deaf-public here. Stick it.

Why is it those with no talent feel the need to skewer those who dare to put themselves out there, hit or miss? You have no idea how much damage you do.

Love Double A. I'm sorry she set that club on fire, and people lost their lives, but this album is not what you say it is. It's actually good!

Double A is no doubt turning over in her grave. Oh, wait. She was cremated. Ain't moldering anywhere you uninformed idiot.

Resurrected discograph? Interesting choice of words since rumor has it Double A has resurrected. Considering she went out in a blaze of revenge, better watch your back.

On that comment Archibald decided to stop reading. He could dish it out, but he wasn't great at taking it. He might be an acid-tongued old cuss, but people made him feel guilty all the time. He just did his best never to show it.

He hobbled from the office, through his bedroom, into an opulent dressing room where a tripod awaited, and attached his phone to the top. On a long counter with double sinks lay a horror mask. He'd wear it when he transformed into the *House of Wax* fiend. Before that, however, his face would serve as a canvas. Top quality stage makeup lay beside the mask. Next to that were realistic-looking hair, beard, and moustache.

Archibald admired his image in the mirror and mentally told himself his eye-bags and wrinkles made him look distinguished, not old. "Handsome fella," he said aloud. He did have a fine-looking face, symmetrical and pleasing to the eye. It might be rounder than Vincent Price's elongated one, but that didn't matter. The makeup artist he'd hired would take care of that.

Archibald switched on the phone's camera, moved to a tall stool, and sat.

"Welcome back, boys and girls, and those whose pronouns change with the wind. Did you enjoy yesterday's tirade about Double A? It certainly allowed me to relieve some stress, although I shan't tell you why. I'm all about secrets today, of which I have many. However, I will share with you that I'm having a party tonight, one it's taken me months to put together. It's been a labor of love and very hush-hush. Now those of you watching this who I count as my very dear friends, don't get your panties in a twist because I didn't invite you. You wouldn't want to be invited to this particular soiree. And I promise to make it up to you by the time Halloween really rolls around. This party is for those who did me wrong, although perhaps only a handful of them are aware that they did that. I keep my feelings very close to my vest, you know."

Archibald laughed.

"That's a lie. I will be releasing this video after ten, so none of my honored guests will see it and decide not to come. I have so many surprises in store for them that I'm certain at least half will have a heart attack." He grinned. "That's the plan anyway."

He paused and gave his next words some thought. "I do want to share with you about one of my invitees, a most special honored guest. I don't think I'll share her name. Maybe I will. No maybe I won't. I won't. At least not now. Forty years ago she not only broke my heart, she sucked the love from my soul. You might say I am who I am today because of her.

"I was twenty-seven at the time and she was eighteen. I was one of the best looking bachelors in town. Such a cutie. A magazine said so, therefore it had to be true." He winked. "The article was titled, *Ten Young, Hot Hollywood Up-and-Comers*. I was lucky number seven.

"It didn't matter though. She told me I was too old for her and I suppose that was true. But I adored her and didn't want to lose her. My career was going well with two hit screenplays under my belt, and I threw it all away. I gave up writing in a disciplined way to give her more time and attention. She was worth it, I thought. For over a year I wrote sporadically and ended up with a heap of rubbish to show for it. My trajectory toward success faltered and when I told her I needed to write in earnest again, she pouted. In the end, I caught her in bed with two of my best friends. She didn't bat an eye or say she was sorry. Instead she taunted me. 'Care to join?' she asked. 'The more the merrier.' She moved out the next day and I was no longer the hot commodity.

"So why am I telling you all this? Three months ago she contacted me. She was doing that twelve-step program we've all heard of, making amends. Every bit of anguish she'd caused flooded back full force. We met and I was disappointed to see that she was still gorgeous at fifty-eight. I'd rather her be a hippo in need of major liposuction with her neck doubled and her face saggy in all the wrong places. Even an over-zealous, half-botched plastic surgery job would have assuaged my desire for payback. If any of this had been the case, I might not have felt the need to invite her to my private Halloween hell."

He wiggled off the stool. "So now, all you pronouns out there, I'm going downstairs and I will record a preview of coming attractions which I know you'll enjoy." He shut off the camera and removed the phone from the tripod.

As Archibald entered the Great Room he found Jordan testing Bessie the skeleton. He had attached her with fishing wire to a temporary ceiling track and was using a remote control to make her move. There was no need for the awkward wooden contraption Vincent Price was shown using in *House on Haunted Hill*. Bessie walked with her own unique gait from a corner of the room toward the center, arms outstretched as in the movie. This was to be the comedy portion of the evening, unless of course someone was a complete wuss.

"What do you think?" Jordan asked. "Pretty cool, huh?"

"*Huh?* You have such a way with words," mocked Archibald. "Let's remove all these sheets and tarps and I'll record you demonstrating the sets."

"No problem," Jordan said.

The young man whipped the sheet from one of the figures too haphazardly for Archibald. "Easy! Each of these pieces cost me a bundle." Jordan nodded and removed the remaining sheets with care to reveal what looked like wax figures from the 1800s and earlier. They included Jack the Ripper and Bluebeard. The most beautiful was Marie Antoinette, dressed in a pale-blue, rococo-style gown. She was a very important wax statue in the *House of Wax* movie. Archibald's Marie Antoinette looked identical to Phyllis Kirk, who played the heroine in the 1953 film.

"I love them," Archibald said. He took a deep breath and exhaled with admiration. The artist he'd hired to make the figures had outdone herself, he thought. "Too bad Marie has to burn."

"A little stiff if you ask me," Jordan replied with a smile. "Get it? Stiff?"

"Yes. I get it."

"Well," Jordan said. "Wait until you see the dummies that *move* with the electronics I designed. Get it? These are stiff, mine move."

"Yes. Yes. Very clever. Now, just a moment." Archibald turned on the camera recorder of his phone, then waved a hand for Jordan to proceed.

Jordan trotted over to a tarp-covered piece and removed the tarp. "Voila!"

The set was simple. A wooden stump had been placed before the figure of Anne Boleyn, who was on her knees. A powerful-looking executioner stood behind her, the top half of his face covered in a black mask with cut-outs for the eyes. He held a long, silver sword in both hands.

"Watch," Jordan said. He pushed a button on the remote. Anne proceeded to lay her head on the stump. The executioner raised the sword and brought it down, stopping just before Anne would lose her head.

Archibald shut off the camera and sighed. "That's fine," he said.

Jordan, expecting more praise, asked, "You don't like it?"

"Of course I like it. It would just be more dramatic and effective if the sword really did its job."

"It's what you asked for."

"I know. I know. Let's move on."

They walked to the next piece and Archibald started to record. Jordan removed the tarp to reveal Joan of Arc on a wood pyre. She looked exactly like the actress Carolyn Jones. She wore a loose gown and was chained to a thick post. Both of her hands held a long staff topped with a large Christian cross. Her glass eyes gazed upon it.

"Ready?" Jordan asked. Archibald nodded and Jordan pressed a button. The wood pyre lit up with gas-jet flames. Nothing caught fire because all the materials were fireproof, but it was still very effective. Archibald stopped recording as Jordan pressed another button, extinguishing the flames. "You like?"

"I like."

Jordan strutted to the next piece and once again Archibald started to record. "Here is the Jean-Paul Marat that you asked for." He removed the tarp. On display was a naked man bathing in a white simulated-porcelain tub, his terrified eyes locked with those of Charlotte Corday, a young woman intent on stopping the French civil war. She wore a gray dress with a white apron, her head covered with a simple, gathered, white mob cap. She stood beside the tub, brandishing a knife. Jordan engaged the electronics and this time the act of murder completed. The knife plunged into a narrow slot in Marat's body, releasing a red liquid that simulated blood. "Nice," Archibald said, pausing the camera.

Jordan stopped the demonstration. "The blood wipes off. You can do it three more times before you're out of capsules."

Archibald nodded. "Very nice. I approve. Next!" he commanded.

Jordan led the way to the last piece. There could have been more, just as in the movie, but Archibald's Great Room, though large, was only so big and he needed space for his guests to mingle. "And last but not least," Jordan said.

"Except for what's outside of the window."

"Except for that." Jordan pulled away the covering. "The guillotine." It was a replica of the efficient killing machine that had executed so many. The figure of a noblewoman knelt over the machine with her hands tied behind her back. Her head lay trapped between two pieces of wood with a circular cutout for the neck. High above hung an angled blade stained with the "blood" of previous victims. An executioner with beefy arms and gloved hands, wearing a crimson robe and full black hood, held the cord that would release the blade. His soulless eyes stared down at the helpless victim. Jordan operated the remote. The executioner pulled the cord and the blade dropped. Quickly decapitated, the woman's head rolled into an awaiting basket.

"The *crème de la crème*," Archibald pronounced.

"The head reattaches so she can be killed again and again. The only drawback, Arch," Jordan said. "I couldn't make it safe. What I mean is, if your guests get drunk and start playing around, someone could lose their head for real. I had to keep the blade sharp. I even cut my hand."

"Hmm," Archibald replied. "Well. Let's hope that happens. Now, the finale."

"This is so cool," Jordan gleefully offered. "Just watch the windows." Both he and Archibald faced the three-windowed wall, the camera on record. Jordan operated the remote and on the yard side of the windows, flames shot into the air, or so it seemed. The blaze fed off gas jets that were secured between two pieces of heat-resistant glass. The trick was perfectly safe, but looked terrifying.

Archibald nodded with approval, then shut off the camera. "My guests will believe they are safe but I'm sure some will race for the exits. Only they'll find the doors locked, which will be cause for alarm."

His eyes shone with anticipation.

"And once I press the buttons, the lights will go out. Marie Antoinette will begin to burn and the funeral pyre for Joan of Arc will blaze away," Jordan said.

Archibald's expression was that of a child in a toy store who is allowed to pick out anything he wants. "They'll think the fire is spreading and everyone should be crazed out of their fucking minds. It will be a mad house. It will be glorious."

Jordan nodded in agreement.

Chapter 2

Pete Ashton pulled his white BMW convertible into the parking garage of his shrink's high rise, found a space away from the elevator where fewer cars crowded the lines, and turned off the engine. He didn't like parking structures for one main reason, the smell, and almost canceled his first appointment with Dr. McKenna because of it. His girlfriend, Robina Winters, had urged him to give the young psychologist a chance. He tended to listen to Robina's advice and was very glad he had.

On the seat beside him lay a dozen yellow roses wrapped in cellophane he'd bought to commemorate the one-year anniversary of therapy. As the saying went, he'd come a long way baby, and wanted to show Dr. McKenna his appreciation. He didn't know if giving your therapist flowers was kosher or not, but he didn't care. If it wasn't, she could refuse them. At least she'd know he was grateful.

Pete had a second surprise for the doctor; he'd cut his hair. A do-it-yourself job for sure, but the results were decent even if he did say so himself. He turned the rearview mirror to properly finger-comb the wavy white locks into submission. He'd driven the freeway with the top down.

Five years. That's how long he'd allowed his hair to grow untamed because he just didn't have the wherewithal to take care of his appearance. After what he called "the event" occurred, he was left a blubbering lump of raw emotion and his once-dark mane turned white in a matter of weeks. His lady-attracting face with the square jaw and expressive green eyes grew gaunt with every meal he refused to eat. Day-to-day living became a burdensome chore which he tried to ease by withdrawing from people. It was left to Robina to make sure he did the things he had to do. She'd say, "Time to rest. Time to eat at least enough to stay alive. Time to pay your bills so you don't get kicked out of this place or have the power turned off. Time to talk to Wayne. He left you a message. It's important."

She stood by him through it all, listening when he cried, when he complained, and when he did nothing but feel sorry for himself. On the days he was undoubtedly legally certifiable, she talked him back to some semblance of sanity, always reassuring him that things would get better. She never grew weary of telling him to remember how fortunate he was. His resources weren't wiped out because the nightclub had been insured to the hilt and he and Wayne did everything above board. Nothing that happened was his fault, so it didn't matter what the press said if it wasn't true. He needed to let the haters hate. He couldn't let the lies that circulated take him down.

Robina held him in her arms throughout the night whenever he needed. She told him she loved him a hundred times a day. She told him she would always be there for him and she meant it. She'd shown him she meant it because in the five years since "the event" she'd never left his side for any length of time.

Pete's business partner, Wayne, had taken on the burden of dealing with the insurance companies, the lawyers, and the media. He hadn't been there the night of the fire and so "the event" hadn't impacted his psyche the way it had Pete's. Wayne was strong, smart, ethical, and compassionate. Pete was lucky to have a person of such good character on his side. He had no doubt if it hadn't been for Robina, Wayne, and Dr. McKenna, he'd be in a wooden box with shiny handles, six feet underground.

Pete checked his Rolex. He was thirty minutes early, which allowed him to heave a relaxed sigh. With L.A. traffic you never knew how long it would take to get where you were going. He always left home with plenty of minutes to spare. Today he left extra early to have time to stop and buy the roses along the way. Pete looked at the flowers with the appreciation of a suitor on Valentine's Day. His loyalty was to Robina, but he did feel a great deal of affection for his therapist. Transference, people called it, possibly even erotic transference, because he could not help but love Dr. McKenna. He was grateful to her, and he did occasionally dream about her, but he didn't pine away. At least she wasn't on his mind twenty-four hours a day. He placed a gentle hand on the bouquet.

See. The roses are yellow, not red.

A car rolled past. Pete wrinkled his nose at the fumes from its exhaust. He could go in and sit in Dr. McKenna's waiting room, but he opted to remain in the car. Other people could be there, and should they be the talkative sort, he didn't want to engage. Despite the progress in his mental health, he still wasn't the outgoing, friendly person he used to be. At thirty-three, the world had been his oyster. At thirty-eight, he was merely doing his best to have a future. At least now he could believe that he had one. He smiled and took a soothing breath.

Thank God for Dr. McKenna. Thank God I decided to open up. Thank God it wasn't five years ago when I was on the brink.

The first two years after "the event," Pete buried himself in his Bel Air home and entertained thoughts of suicide. He didn't go anywhere. The only people he spoke to were Robina and Wayne. Finally Wayne issued an ultimatum. Get help! Go to therapy or he was going to find a way to have him committed. That prodded Pete enough to at least go through the motions, and he turned the process into a game.

Pete found therapists with the highest accolades. He decided to see how good they were at figuring out the truth. He didn't provide his real name and shared fictional horror stories about his past. Sometimes he told them he'd been abducted by aliens. Sometimes he told them he was a victim of child abuse. Sometimes he confessed he was a convicted murderer on the lam to see how frightened they'd become. Three months was about how long Pete spent with each doctor before the jig was up. They would come to realize that he was full of shit, and although they'd be willing to continue taking his money hoping he would change his ways, they would only smile and nod at anything he said.

That's when Pete would quit, take a break from head doctors, and finally confess to Wayne he was therapist-free. Wayne would insist that he seek help and the process would begin all over again.

Dr. McKenna was therapist number four. Pete had chosen her at random. She didn't have a slew of degrees or a ton of awards and she had been in practice for a mere two years, but Pete found her so genuine, so concerned, he felt like a caged animal set free while in her presence. After only three sessions he told her his real name and shared what was really going on in his life.

He told her about Andrea, his sister. She tried to kill him by setting fire to a nightclub he owned while he was inside. Ten people died, including Andrea.

Pete remembered that he'd paused before sharing the next bit. Even now, a year later, it made his heart race to think of the moment he'd finally spewed. Tears filled his eyes the way water overwhelmed a sinking ship.

"My sister," he'd told her, "blames me for her death. She haunts me. Not just in my dreams, but in real life. My sister is a ghost who is doing her best to drive me to the funny farm. I probably am insane, but I swear on a stack of Bibles I've seen her."

Dr. McKenna had not batted an eye and Pete didn't know if she believed him or not, but he continued explaining that the first time Andrea appeared to him was in the hospital where he'd been taken for smoke inhalation. Her ghost floated beside his bed, looking as she did when she died.

He didn't share the gory details about her appearance. He didn't want to gross Dr. McKenna out. He sat in the chair across from her as pictures of that night assaulted his brain. He saw Andrea freshly dead, stinking of gasoline, smoldering on the sidewalk in front of the seething nightclub. No longer beautiful, no longer vital, she was a hideous, revolting corpse more sickening than a Wes Craven monster. Her face was charred black with bits of skull showing where the flames had burned through to the bone. Red pools of blood glistened on the blackened skin, having seeped from her nose and mouth. Her teeth were exposed in a weird, contorted grimace probably caused by searing pain.

"Ten dead," he'd told Dr. McKenna, "and everyone said it could have been worse. But I don't think so. Ten is ten too many. She may have paid the ultimate price, but I hate Andrea for what she did."

Two cars and a loud, souped-up truck passed by his parked car in succession, tires squealing as they turned into the next row. Pete winced. It seemed to him the smell of fumes had intensified. He pushed the idea away.

I'm imagining it. It's because I'm thinking about that night. I'm thinking about Andrea. Get a grip. Get a grip.

Pete hadn't smelled Andrea's signature gasoline scent for almost a year, not since practicing Dr. McKenna's techniques to stay in the present.

He checked his watch again. It was twenty minutes until two. Still too early, but he thought it might be better to take himself out of the parking garage and ride the elevator up to the ninth floor. His thoughts flip-flopped like a teeter-totter.

Encounter strangers or smell the fumes?

The elevator won. He scooped up the roses, then reached for the door handle just as he happened to glance in the mirror. His heart leapfrogged into his throat and he froze. Andrea gazed back at him. It didn't matter that she no longer appeared as the gruesome corpse splayed on the sidewalk, she shouldn't be in the backseat of his car. The sight filled him with terror. His blood froze. His gullet squeezed shut. He couldn't even shout at the hallucination to go away. Sweat appeared on his brow. His heart beat faster and faster.

This is how Jack the Ripper's victims would have felt if they'd had time to think before the thrusting of the blade.

Andrea continued to stare. Her unblinking gaze seemed to be a warning. In his mind he heard her say, *Go no further.* He pictured one of those signs: *In case of flood turn around, don't drown.*

Go no further? She didn't want him visiting Dr. McKenna? What? Why? Why now?

Go away! he cried in his head, his blood pulsing in his ears. *Now!*

The image of Andrea remained steadfast.

He dropped the roses on the passenger seat and rubbed his knuckles into his eye sockets. That should work. Rub hard enough and you rub her out.

Rub a dub dub. Rub a dub dub. Take control and scrub, scrub, scrub.

Pete found his voice. "Andrea. I know you aren't really there. You're something I used to conjure up when my subconscious couldn't accept what you'd done. I don't need that anymore. Dr. McKenna taught me to accept what happened. So, I ask you, no I direct you, stay away. Don't start up again."

He removed his hands and took a look. She was grinning at him, charred and burned, gruesome and monstrous. His throat opened wide and he screamed and screamed until tears ran down his cheeks. He fought to find the door handle, hands slapping in the air.

Suddenly she was gone. His terror lessened. His heart began to quiet down even though his chest continued to heave. At least she was gone. Thank God, she was gone.

But why had she come at all? He'd been doing so well. What had made her show up now? He didn't know. He'd discuss it with Dr. McKenna. Yes, that's what he'd do. She would have answers and he'd get back on track.

He reached for the roses and froze again. They had withered into little balls. They looked like shriveled testicles exposed to cold on an icy winter's day.

Chapter 3

The house was very still. Archibald had edited the footage he'd videoed earlier and scheduled it to premier on his website at midnight. The makeup artist had come and gone. Jordan had left with Remy to eat dinner somewhere. Marta was taking a nap in a room on the third floor. The "extras" he had hired to stand around in costume and come alive at opportune moments wouldn't arrive for over an hour.

Wearing the Victorian suit, Archibald admired himself in his cheval mirror. He wouldn't say he looked like Vincent Price, but he had his style. The hair and goatee were perfect, as was the costume. For a few seconds he bent his body and ambled about the bedroom, feet pigeon-toed in a perfect imitation of the *House of Wax* fiend. Archibald tossed on the smock. It didn't matter if the smock got dirty before the festivities began. It was an artist's smock and had imitation paint and clay smears all over the front.

He wasn't hungry. He was too excited. The party wasn't going to start until ten p.m., when it was good and dark outside. Right now it was only a quarter past seven. He decided to go downstairs and take another look around the Great Room. He wanted to savor his creation before everyone showed up.

Archibald turned on the lights as he stepped into the party space. All of the figures looked appropriately creepy, with eyes that seemed to follow him. He'd told the artist to make their faces slightly evil.

He wanted the malevolence to be present enough to make his guests think, *I'm glad that isn't a real person, but what if it is?*

He wondered for a moment if he should have stuck with just one movie theme, obviously *House of Wax*. But locking the partygoers in for the night as in *House on Haunted Hill* was a nice touch, he decided. It would create a feeling of unease. Maybe having blood drip from the ceiling was over the top, but it was fun. No one liked having some unknown substance on their skin. He peered at the center of the ceiling where a large circular spot had been stained red. Jordan had installed a hidden mechanism that would release droplets of red liquid on command. Some lucky guest would be manipulated to the middle of the room and receive the full effect. As for the skeleton, Archibald was having second thoughts. No one would think a walking skeleton was real and it would make everyone laugh. But was that what he really wanted? Maybe he'd nix that.

He glanced toward a dark corner of the room where a screen hid Bessie. As he debated with himself, he became aware of the noxious smell of gasoline, the odor so overwhelming he coughed and covered his nose.

What the hell's going on? Had Jordan rigged up some smell machine Archibald hadn't asked for? He wouldn't put it past the little bastard.

Unexpectedly, the entrance doors to the Great Room slammed shut and Archibald jerked with a start. Simultaneously the screen fell over, revealing Bessie. She sat slumped in the corner looking like something to be rescued. Inexplicably, the lights went out and Archibald's heart skipped a beat. Outside, it was edging toward dusk. Because of the windows, the room wasn't dark, but it was sufficiently gloomy to be creepy.

"Jordan, are you back?" Archibald coughed. "Marta, did you slam the doors?"

Why would she? Why would he? Archibald was mystified. His gaze swept from one wax figure to another until he came back to Bessie. She was no longer slumped, but sitting upright.

No, thought Archibald. *That can't be right. I must be remembering wrong.*

He stared because he knew he wasn't. The skeleton was definitely in a different position. He took a step back and was suddenly overcome with another hit of gasoline. With his hand over his nose, he hobbled to an exit. It was best to get the hell out of there until Jordan showed up. The kid had some explaining to do.

Archibald pulled on the door, but it remained firmly locked in place. He tried the second exit with the same result. "Jordan!" he yelled.

His lungs burned. *Jesus,* he thought.

Cough . . . cough . . . cough.

He banged a fist on his chest, hoping that would help. When he recovered enough from the coughing jag, he called out again. "Jordan! Damn you! I know you're here!"

No sound came from the other side of the door, but the speakers suddenly came alive with Double A's music. He twisted on his heels and limped away from the doors. This was stupid. This was beyond stupid. Jordan was playing a joke. It had to be. He was . . .

Archibald spotted the remote placidly lying on the appetizer table. He swallowed in an effort to steady his nerves as he shuffled toward the table and picked it up. He had no idea which button to push to shut off the speakers. He needed Jordan for that.

"Jordan!" he screamed, causing another bout of coughing.

The music cut out. *What now?* He heard a noise and his eyes darted toward the corner again. Bessie was standing, one foot in front of the other, as if she'd been walking.

"That's impossible," whispered Archibald. He stared, daring her to take another step. She didn't budge. He suddenly laughed. Feeling emboldened, he asked, "Why don't you move when I'm watching?"

Because it's scarier when I don't see.

His eyes twinkled. If Jordan wanted to play games, he'd play games. He zigzagged and twirled in a lame sort of fashion to the center of the room.

But I'm not scared. You can't scare me. I set this up. This is my creation.

"Do you hear me, Jordan? You can't scare me!"

Cough... cough... cough...

He bent over, the cough coming from deep within his chest. His hand clung tightly to the remote as if it were sustenance. But then a stinging, searing pain splashed his skin and he dropped it, screaming in agony and moving aside. Tears filled his eyes as he looked at his hand. Something red and caustic had dripped on it and was now hitting the floor with a sizzle. He wiped his hand on the smock but it still burned like the devil. The skin began to blister. He looked up at the ceiling where Jordan was supposed to have rigged fake blood, but had used some caustic liquid instead. Archibald was livid. Words caught in his throat.

You motherfucker, Jordan! When I get my hands on you...

He heard something akin to footsteps behind him, distracting him from the pain. With his heart doing its best to jump out of his chest, he turned. Two of the dummies, Bluebeard and Jack the Ripper, had inched closer. He could swear they were grinning at him. The smell of gasoline intensified.

"Stay where you are!" he barked at the figures, laughing at his stupidity, crying in pain. Inhaling what could only be gas fumes, he coughed some more.

I sound like an idiot. There must be another remote. Jordan did more electronic work than I asked for and he's hiding somewhere.

"Jordan!"

Archibald stepped backward, away from the grinning pair, until he tripped over something on the floor. He grabbed for the nearest object to keep from falling, a support post from the guillotine. The noblewoman dummy lay crumpled on the floor. He couldn't remember if she'd been like that when he entered the room, but he didn't think so. No longer concerned with how much these figures had cost him, he kicked her out of the way.

Archibald leaned against the guillotine post for support. He was out of breath from exertion and fear. He rested, taking long deep breaths. Kicking the dummy had taken a lot out of him.

He heard a step and looked up. Bessie wasn't moving, but she was also closer, maybe eight feet away. Archibald shook his head. He was wrong. A walking skeleton wasn't funny at all. He wanted to cry.

Suddenly Joan of Arc's pyre flared. He half expected the room to explode into flames. Thank goodness it didn't, but Marie Antoinette ignited and that was a catastrophe. She would be destroyed. He looked for the remote which had bounced out of sight and stared helplessly at his beloved Marie Antoinette as she burned. Her fair complexion melted and she morphed into a freakish, hellish sight.

The fire burned. Marie Antoinette melted. Double A's music returned. Then all at once everything came alive. Anne Boleyn's executioner sliced at her neck, again and again. Marat was murdered with a strike of Charlotte Corday's knife, over and over. And Archibald felt two powerful hands grasp his upper arms. The French executioner had hold of him. Archibald fought with every ounce of his strength. But it did no good. The executioner was too strong. Archibald was pushed down onto the guillotine and his head was locked in place between the two pieces of wood with the half-moon cutouts. Icy terror shot through his veins. Instead of facing the ground, Archibald was looking up at the guillotine blade. He screamed as he pounded on the scaffold.

A woman's laughter filled the room.

"Help me!" Archibald shrieked as something strapped his wrists so he could no longer use his hands.

The woman laughed louder and louder, but at the same time seemed to cry as if she were a wounded animal.

"Please! Please!!" Archibald screamed hysterically until tears trickled down the sides of his temples. He squeezed the lids closed, crying. "Oh, please." When he opened his eyes they went large and round, as big as silver dollars.

"There's nothing I could do," a woman's voice whispered in his ear.

The last thing Archibald saw was the sharp, shiny blade racing toward his neck.

Chapter 4

Dr. McKenna, Harmony to her friends, savored a medium-bodied Merlot in her favorite Italian bistro while she waited for her beau and best friend, Jesse. It was after nine. He'd texted to say he was sorry. He was running late. He'd be there as soon as he could, and he'd make it up to her. He'd pay for dinner. It was a bit of a joke. He always paid for dinner. She sighed. Jesse often ran late, and thirty-five minutes wasn't a record, but she'd had a trying afternoon and needed a shoulder to cry on. Sitting alone, wondering when he'd show, made her feel worse.

She took a sip of the Merlot and glanced around. The smell of enticing Italian spices infused the air. It was Saturday night and the restaurant was filled with couples in the mood for romance. It was that kind of place. Soft music. Muted lighting. White linen tablecloths and golden candles. Dozens of wine bottles lay in wooden racks built into the walls. Tables were square and seated two to six people. The space had been designed for intimacy.

Families were welcome, although they tended to show early, around five, and be gone by this time. Tonight one family straggled. A couple with a well-behaved little girl, around the age of six, sat nearby. Harmony supposed they hadn't been able to find a sitter. She lifted her glass to her lips, and with the acoustics the way they were, easily heard the mother whisper, "Honey, don't stare. It's impolite." Harmony gave the child a glance and realized the little girl was looking at her. She offered a smile, but the girl didn't react. The mother grimaced apologetically at Harmony. "I'm sorry," she said, putting a hand on her child's arm, drawing her attention back to their table.

"It's fine," Harmony said. "She's adorable."

"Thank you. It's our anniversary. The sitter cancelled."

Harmony sighed. She knew what had attracted the little girl's attention. Her scar. A narrow river of blushing pink curved alongside her cheekbone, down to her chin. Years ago, a man had tried to kill her. The scar had healed as much as it was going to, but it remained highly visible. The slit scar on her throat where he'd started to slash, but was interrupted, was smaller and not as noticeable. The stab wounds on her chest were hidden by clothing, of course.

She finished her glass of Merlot and was no longer hungry. Leaving a mostly-full bottle of wine on the table, she stood and reached for her pocketbook when Jesse rushed in.

"Apologies, my love." He kissed her cheek. "I'm so sorry. You look beautiful, as always. Sit. Sit."

He never failed to compliment her which made it hard to stay mad. Harmony sat. She didn't ask why he was tardy. He was a therapist, just as she was, and he always gave the same excuse: unexpected late-evening client.

"I'm famished." He poured wine into his glass and replenished hers. Their server immediately appeared. His name was Richard. He was in his early thirties, gay, and had a flaming crush on Jesse which he never tried to hide.

"Hello," Richard greeted as he placed warm bread on the table. "You've left your lovely lady sitting all alone for far too long. We're so glad you've arrived."

Jesse had a smile that could light up a room. He was six-foot five, muscular, and dressed impeccably—never a t-shirt or jeans. Only name-brand slacks and form-fitting shirts suited him. "How are you tonight, Richard?" he asked.

"Better, now that you're here. Are you having the usual?"

Jesse looked at Harmony. She'd definitely lost her appetite. But she's the one who'd insisted on dinner and if she didn't order something, it wouldn't be right. She supposed she could always box dinner up and take it home. "Cheese ravioli."

"So, it is the usual," Jesse said. "Spaghetti with clams."

"My favorite, as well," Richard responded. As if they didn't already know. "Will you be needing another bottle?"

"I don't think so," Harmony said, cutting Jesse off before he could answer.

"I guess not." Jesse's eyes smiled at Richard.

"Okay. Cuisine coming right up." Richard departed.

Jesse drew a deep breath and blew it out with a sigh. He was hyper and needed to calm himself. In the old days, people would have reached for a cigarette. *He must have had a big breakthrough with a client*, Harmony thought.

"So you insisted on dinner this evening. Something happen? I really do apologize for being late." He sipped from his wine glass and frowned. He checked the label on the bottle. "Not my favorite."

"Nope. It's mine."

"Oh. Passive-aggressive, I see."

Harmony didn't correct him. He was right. She knew he'd be late and she was honestly getting tired of it. She'd been challenging him of late. He didn't complain, but he knew.

"Well. I deserve it for being late," he said as he smiled.

The sound of chairs scraping on the wooden floor drew Harmony's attention. The family with the child stood up to leave. The little girl didn't hesitate. She took her short, small legs over to Harmony, leaned in, and in a loud whisper said, "I'm sorry I stared. I think you're pretty."

"Ahhh," Harmony responded. "Thank you. I think you're pretty, too."

The family walked on, the mother wishing Harmony a good night.

"Your scar?" Jesse asked, sliding a finger down the side of his face.

"For a short while it was the main attraction."

"You wear it well," Jesse said. He reached across the table for her hands and they clasped fingers.

Harmony rarely thought about the scars on her body and when she did, she put a positive spin on it. If it hadn't been for the knife attack six years earlier, *she* might have been at Peter's hotspot when it burned down. She'd been attracted to trendy clubs in her twenties. Letting loose on the dance floor had been her thing. She'd met husband number two dancing—a real hottie with a roving eye. Their marriage lasted all of three months.

She took a lot of chances in those days. Buying weed in dark alleys. Leaving clubs with complete strangers to party until dawn. Drinking so much other people had to look after her, people who drank too much themselves. Funny how it wasn't risky behavior that nearly got her killed. She'd been walking to her car in broad daylight when a complete stranger threw her to the ground and went to work carving up her face, chest, and neck. Then just as he was about to deliver the *coups de grace*, another stranger interrupted him. If he'd slit her throat first, she wouldn't have attracted attention with her screams. But, she suspected, the attacker wanted her alive and terrified for a while before he finished her off. The monster was never found. Even if he'd been caught she wouldn't have been able to identify him. His face was masked and she'd been so busy fighting for her life she didn't really see much. However, she would know him by his smell. He wore distinctive cologne, too much of it. If she ever encountered it again, she'd know it was him. She told the police about his stinky scent and it made the news.

Sometimes the bad things that happened in one's life turned out to be for the best. She changed her dangerous ways and met Jesse while recovering in the hospital. He'd come to visit a friend. His friend, as it turned out, had already been released and when he glanced into Harmony's room as he walked down the hall, he saw her sitting up, eating, bandages on her face and neck. Never shy, he walked right in and sympathetically asked her what happened.

Harmony could hardly believe such brazen behavior. She tried to tell him it was none of his business, to go away. But Jesse, being Jesse, didn't listen. Instead, he somehow put her at ease and she opened up about her close call with death. It was Jesse who put her on the path to become a psychotherapist. Prior to that, she'd been studying to be a teacher.

The pair had been exclusive for six years with no marriage date in sight. Each had their own place with occasional sleepovers. The arrangement suited both of them. No one pushed for a change. Harmony had been married and divorced twice by the age of twenty-four and wasn't eager for another possible failure. She was now thirty-four. Jesse was forty-six. He had never tied the knot.

"What are you thinking about, my love?" Jesse asked.

Harmony realized she'd been lost in thought and he'd been studying her. "Oh. You. Me. Life in general."

"Ah. Is that all?" He smiled. "So. Why was dinner so imperative? Tell me about your day."

Harmony shook her head. "No need now. I feel better. I think that little girl made all the difference."

"And not me?" He pretended to look offended.

She chuckled. "It's nothing, really. Just a no-show. But when I tried to call, I got nowhere. No answer. No call back. I started to worry. It bothered me. Did something happen? Is there something I should know?"

The teasing twinkle in Jesse's eyes faded. "You've had no-shows before. You've had clients walk out calling you a bitch, even an asshole."

"I know."

"But this one's different," he said. "This is—how should I put it? Your special case." He withdrew his fingers and his face took on the look he gave when he wasn't pleased.

"I'd be upset about any of my clients not returning my calls. But of all my clients he's the most vulnerable. I really am afraid he might harm himself. Anyway, I have this odd, perplexing feeling—like I know— he isn't coming back."

"Good."

"Jesse. Why do you say that?"

"Because even though you haven't told me anything about him—you've been an ethical therapist towing that doctor-client privilege line—I can tell when you're thinking about him."

"If you knew his situation, I think he'd take up space in your head, too."

"Well. There's a way to find out. Ask him if you can consult with me about him. He'll probably say yes. Then we'll know."

Harmony shrugged. "I asked before. He wasn't keen on the idea. Remember?"

Jesse's eyes bored into her. "It doesn't matter. I know who he is."

"You don't. I never told you."

"You talk in your sleep." He lifted his glass as if toasting to an important reveal and took a drink.

Harmony kept watch for a tell Jesse had. When he lied he would wipe his upper lip with his index finger. She didn't see him do it.

Richard arrived with dinner. He always delivered their food personally, never using a runner. He smiled at both of them, although his eyes lingered on Jesse. "*Buon appetito!*" he said.

"*Grazie*, Richard," Jesse said.

Harmony said, "Can I have a box?"

***

Pete lay in a fetal position on Darius' over-large beanbag lounger. It was nine-thirty at night. He'd been asleep for hours. After calling Robina and leaving a message on the home phone explaining where he was going, he'd come straight to Darius' apartment for solace. Darius wasn't a therapist, or even a friend. He was a self-proclaimed psychic medium whose calm demeanor, chants, and prayers calmed

Pete down when he was in crisis. Pete also thought it didn't hurt that Darius gave him anti anxiety medicine. He had found him through a small ad that Darius had placed online looking for clients. This was during the period when Pete was playing games, lying to licensed therapists.

Pete opened his eyes. It took him a minute to realize where he was. He hadn't run to Darius in months, not since he started to get results from his sessions with Dr. McKenna. But today it was as if he'd been slammed in the stomach with a sledgehammer. Seeing Andrea's ghost again was just more than he could handle. Did her appearance mean all of Dr. McKenna's counseling was bullshit?

Robina leaned over him. "You're awake."

Pete blinked. He turned his head and saw Darius sitting cross-legged in meditation on the floor. He was a tall man with long, dark, wavy hair and a full beard, around thirty-five years of age. He wore billowy white pants and a soft pastel pink tunic. Around his neck were beads as well as gold chains of varying lengths.

On the door to Darius' office was a plaque that read: *Namaste*. Lamplight painted everything with a soft, soothing glow. Bookshelves were cluttered with parapsychology books mixed haphazardly with spiritual and new age material. One shelf contained dozens of decks of Oracle and Tarot cards. A small table supported Tibetan singing bowls. Crystals and rocks, polished and unpolished, could be found all over the room. A small wicker basket clearly labeled with the word DONATIONS sat on a wooden stool beside the door. There was also a bowl filled with stones that acted as a water fountain.

Inspirational posters on the walls offered Darius' clients words of wisdom:

Your only limit is your mind.

Strive for progress not perfection. What you think you become. What you feel you attract. What you imagine you create. – Buddha

If your compassion does not include yourself, it is incomplete. – Buddha

Darius was a mishmash of beliefs. Neither Pete nor Robina believed he was a psychic medium. Pete had played his game with Darius the way he had with the well-accoladed shrinks. One thing he'd done different. He'd shared that he was seeing a ghost, but didn't say who she was. In short, Darius was left in the dark and never seemed to catch on. That didn't necessarily make him a fraud. He had taken lots of classes and seminars, ones on mediumship, the teachings of Ram Dass, dream therapy, spiritual awakening, healing and wellness with your mind. All were attested to by the certificates of completion amid the inspirational posters on the walls. More importantly, Darius also had diplomas from colleges of divinity: one from a university in India and one from Harvard. Pete maintained his suspicions about Darius, however. None of the certificates or diplomas included dates.

Darius spoke without opening his eyes. "Has your panic attack passed?"

"I think so," Pete replied. "The Xanax helped."

Darius smiled. "Perhaps it is time to tell you, I only provide placebos. The mind is a very powerful thing." He stood up and sat in an office chair. He gazed at Pete. "Did you dream?"

Pete had to think. "Not that I recall."

"Dreams can help a lot. As I said before, you should keep a journal."

"If I can't remember them, what's the point?"

"You'll start remembering them. You could have a dream that tells you why your ghost came back. You told me that's what set off your panic."

"If you're a psychic medium, why can't you just tell me?" He wasn't being snarky. He genuinely wanted to know what Darius would say to the honest question.

"I could. But what's the good of that?"

"I'd have my answer."

"The answer lies within."

Pete knew he wasn't going to get anywhere playing one-upmanship. At least he felt rested. He never slept that well at home. He glanced over at Robina, who sat on a love seat away from Pete and Darius. She must have stayed with him the entire time.

Darius placed the back of his hands on his knees and closed his eyes. He began to do the simple OM chant. Pete closed his eyes and joined him.

Ooooommmm . . .

Chapter 5

It was late. As the partygoers cooled their heels in the library, the police combed the crime scene for clues to what exactly happened to Archibald Bent.

Police Detective Donato Guerrero, dressed in his customary gray woolen suit, meadow green shirt, and silk paisley tie, sidestepped the executioner as he took his two-hundred-fifty-pound body on a stroll around the guillotine that had taken Archibald Bent's life. The headless body still lay on the platform, hands strapped down at the wrists. Detective Gunnar Berry stood nearby, arms crossed, a look of disinterest on his face. Rumor had it young Berry was looking to leave Robbery Homicide and it showed. He didn't like being called in on murder cases at all hours, day and night. Guerrero couldn't fault him for that. It was also rumored that Berry thought the dead visited in his sleep because his dreams were so vivid and he couldn't take it anymore.

"So what do you think? Suicide maybe?" Berry asked, looking away.

Guerrero eyed the restraints. "How could he restrain his hands and pull the release cord?"

Berry stared at Archibald's wrists. "I dunno. He was playing around, slipped his hands through the straps, the blade fell by accident, and whammo." Berry karate-chopped the palm of one hand.

"Still not suicide."

"No. It wouldn't be." Berry sniffed.

The young cop's dismissive manner was baffling considering the out-of-the-ordinary way Archibald Bent died. Perhaps the dead didn't like Berry's attitude and really did haunt his dreams. The thought was fleeting. Guerrero didn't believe it for a second because he didn't believe in an afterlife.

The veteran detective looked in the basket. Archibald's head lay face up with wide-open eyes in an expression of terror. He'd been afraid all right. Guerrero turned away. It wasn't a pretty sight. Blood had spurted and made a sticky mess. He'd been a policeman for thirty years, a detective for nineteen of them, and had never grown used to the gore.

Guerrero glanced at the coroner and nodded that he'd finished. Photos had been taken, and the coroner had already examined what he could. He motioned for two attendants to take the victim to the morgue.

"Bring the basket," the coroner directed.

They unstrapped Archibald and placed him in a body bag. Then they wheeled him out on a gurney. A busy CSI team remained, continuing their pursuit of evidence.

"Well?" asked Berry.

"You got some place to be?" Guerrero asked.

Berry shrugged.

Guerrero made a mental note to see if he could get someone else assigned to help him with what had to be a case of murder. He rubbed his face and neck. Although, not wanting to jump the gun, he put forth the theory the death might have been an accident if Mr. Bent had been joking around with someone. He rested his chin against a knuckle, gazed at the guillotine, and reflected.

However it happened, what a bizarre way to go.

Guerrero glanced at the two separate entrance doors and decided the CSIs would need to figure out what happened there. How had they closed? How had they locked from the outside? Did someone murder the guy, leave, and simply lock the doors? The kid who discovered the body said the doors were closed and he had to unlock them. He used a key Archibald Bent had given him so he could come and go.

"This one should be a breeze," Berry said, his eyes chasing upward to the security cameras. "There're four of 'em."

"I saw," Guerrero said.

"I guess Bent wanted to record his party for posterity. Too bad he'll never enjoy the footage."

"Yes. That's what's too bad." Guerrero left the sarcasm in his voice, but Berry didn't appear to notice, or if he had, didn't mind. "Except for the kid who found the victim and made the animatronics, I have all the party people in the library. We might as well let 'em go since we have their info. None arrived until after Bent was found. Oh, except for Remy. She needs to come to the station Monday and make a statement. And Marta. She was here but said she heard nothing. We still need her statement. Go and tell them they can leave, then you might as well leave, too."

"Cool," Berry said. He strutted out, adjusting the knot of his tie.

Guerrero lumbered into the hall and motioned for Jordan to join him. Standing together at the entrance to the party room, the cop gestured with a sweep of his hand. "So, to be clear, you set all this up."

"I didn't make the dummies. I made the sets and the electronic devices that worked the dummies. Everything operated by remote control."

"The doors, too?"

"Well, yeah. Archie wanted them to slam shut on their own and scare his guests."

Guerrero nodded. "And lock."

"Yep. If you go on Archie's website you can see how this stuff works. Maybe not the doors. I don't remember him recording that. But go to Archibaldsbenttalk.com. He filmed most of it and made a video."

"Did he film the guillotine in operation?"

"Yeah. I'm pretty sure."

"And you built the guillotine."

"Yes. But it had a dummy in it. The dummy was supposed to lose her head. Go on the website. I don't have a clue why Archie would put his head in there. I warned him the blade was sharp."

"You must think he did this to himself."

"Well, how else?" Jordan looked wide-eyed, which made Guerrero suspicious.

"Oh, I don't know. You look like a healthy young man. Mr. Bent, as I understand, walked with a limp and was arthritic. Maybe he didn't want to pay you what you were due. Maybe you had a fight. Maybe you killed him in the heat of the moment."

"No, sir. I told you before. I was out to dinner when this happened. I was with Remy. Yes, I found him. *We* found him. We found him already dead. Look at the videos from the cameras I set up in there. And he'd already paid me. Thank God. Besides. I liked Archie. He was funny. A lot of people didn't like him, I know. But I really did think he was cool. I mean, who thinks up a party like this? Archie, that's who."

"Is there more than one remote?"

The corners of Jordan's mouth turned down, providing the slightest indication that the question was unexpected. He gave a truncated shake of the head. "No."

"And that's the truth," the detective prodded.

With an index finger Jordan slashed an X on his chest like a little boy. "Cross my heart and hope to die."

The detective sighed. "All right, Jordan. Come to the station on Monday and we'll take your official statement."

"Great." Jordan turned for the foyer. Glancing over his shoulder, he scurried away before the big cop could change his mind.

Detective Guerrero ambled into the party room and gave it one last turn. He snorted at the display of wax figures and sets. He had to make do on a civil servant's salary while rich men like Archibald Bent spent money on posh parties like this. Ah, well. It was his money. But what else might he have accomplished with it, Guerrero thought.

He looked at the melted Marie Antoinette, totally unrecognizable now, and shook his head. What a mess. Who would have wanted to hurt this rich old man? That was the sixty-four million dollar question. The cop had been informed sixty-four million was how much Archibald Bent was worth. Maybe someone was in line to get rich and moved up the delivery date. Perhaps, Guerrero thought, he'd get lucky and the answer would be in the footage from the cameras Jordan had installed. Wouldn't that be a kick in the pants? This case, his curtain call before retirement, gets solved in a matter of hours. He could hope. Nah. He was never that lucky. But man, what a strange case to go out on.

One of the CSIs handed Guerrero a thumb drive with footage from the cameras. "The news isn't great," the young woman told him. "Outside cameras, shut down. Four cameras in here, three of them recorded nothing. The fourth one is not directed at the guillotine and it's grainy. We should be able to clean it up, but I don't think it caught your killer."

"*Gracias*," Guerrero said. He plodded out the door. He would head back to the station and take a look at the footage. He'd also check out Bent's website. It didn't matter that it was after midnight, Sunday morning now. Guerrero was a night owl and he had no one to go home to.

Chapter 6

Early Sunday morning Harmony drove her blue Kia hybrid from her house in Woodland Hills to Manhattan Beach to people-watch, get some exercise, and occupy her mind. A mental health day, she called it—a day on her own without Jesse.

Her first order of business was to find an open-air café where she enjoyed a cup of coffee and a lemon scone. The sky was overcast and the weather cool, but by eleven the temperature was supposed to warm up to a comfortable seventy degrees. She could see patches of blue sky already doing their best to break through the sullen gray.

When she finished her coffee she strolled along the beachfront walkway called the Strand. Activity continued to pick up as the minutes ticked by with people jogging, walking dogs, biking, and skating. Young people played beach volleyball using city-provided nets that dotted the sand.

Harmony reached the pier and walked to the end where an octagonal building stood. It housed an aquarium that wasn't open. Men and women caught mackerel all along the pier with fishing poles rigged with multiple hooks. They dropped their squirmy catches into buckets, then cast their lines for more. Dolphins dove through the sea as an occasional swimmer free-styled past. The day was idyllic. None of the beachgoers seemed to have a care in the world.

Harmony knew that couldn't be true. Everyone had issues. Even if this day was perfect, tomorrow could bring tragedy. Look at Peter. On top of the world one moment, his life and psyche forever altered the next. To be so successful and have it all: a songwriting career, a nightclub with celebrity clientele, to be a bit of a celebrity himself... and to lose it all because his sister had gone off her rocker. *Wow. Just wow.*

He must have relapsed. Missing his appointment with no explanation continued to bother her. She thought he'd turned a corner, that therapy had helped him that much, that *she* had helped him that much.

She leaned against the pier railing and caught sight of a momma seal and her baby gliding through the water. They disappeared below the surface and reappeared several times before dropping from sight, remaining beneath the pier.

Harmony looked up at the sky. The gray had dissipated and billowy white clouds drifted ever so slightly. It made her think of Peter again, with his long white hair. His face really had become less haunted, less emaciated, under her care. He was more the Peter he used to be, the successful songwriter-nightclub owner she'd seen in magazines before the fire. Even with the sadness that lingered in his eyes, anyone could see he had greatly improved. He was even better adept at handling the criticisms in the press. Accusations had lessened over the years, but on the anniversaries of the fire, journalists with nothing original to write about would dredge up Peter's story and repeat things like: "Sources tell us Pete Ashton knows he's to blame." "Double A was made a scapegoat." "Authorities may reinvestigate."

Oh, stop! Get out of your head. You came to the beach for a change of pace, not to think about Peter.

Harmony walked a couple of miles to a bike rental store she'd found online and rented an E-bike. She rode to Venice Beach, something she and Jesse often did early in their relationship when they'd been thick as thieves. She missed those days. It seemed to her that their interaction had become routine and lazy. Not only that, she felt he'd become increasingly controlling. It might be he'd always demonstrated that trait and she'd missed it. Love is blind and all that.

She could have invited him to come with her to the beach today, but hadn't. She was still miffed that he hadn't told her she talked in her sleep. Even worse, he'd lorded it over her. He'd been condescending.

As she rode back to Manhattan Beach, she began to soften. It wasn't Jesse's fault she talked. She should have asked him to join her. A day spent together like this might have helped to reignite the spark that had brought them together in the first place. She pulled to the side of the bike path, stopped riding, and found her phone. She texted Jesse to let him know she was thinking of him.

After she returned the bike, Harmony found a restaurant where she enjoyed some fish and chips, and then drove home.

That night, Harmony watched shadows sway on the bedroom ceiling as she lay in her queen-sized bed, unable to sleep. It was a breezy night and one of the curtains was slightly ajar. Moonlight played hide-and-seek with the branches of the backyard mulberry tree.

Peter reentered her thoughts and she chased the thoughts away. So, he'd been a no-show. She'd had no-shows before, just as Jesse said.

Stop thinking and go to sleep, she told herself. *You'll drive yourself crazy.*

She closed her eyes and began to drift when the doorbell rang. She rose onto her elbows and listened. Someone turned the lock and entered the house.

Jesse.

After a few seconds he appeared in her bedroom. "It's after midnight, I know. Did I wake you? I called, but you must have left your phone in your purse again."

"I must have. It's in the living room. I didn't hear," Harmony confessed.

"I was happy to get your text. I took it to mean you're no longer mad at me." He sat on the edge of the bed.

"I'm not. But I need to learn to not talk in my sleep."

He straddled her then leaned down and gently kissed her. "I don't mind. That way I get to learn what's whirring through that gorgeous little head."

She plucked at his shirt. "I mind, if I'm talking about my clients."

He lifted her chin and they began to kiss. He pulled off his shirt and threw it aside. They stared into each other's eyes and for the first time Harmony detected a look she hadn't seen before. It was strange and animalistic. It was as if he were hungry for her because he needed to prove something. It was an odd thing to think. It bothered her, but she dismissed it. They began to kiss more intently and she surrendered to the moment. They held each other and touched each other. He wasn't rough, but he was strong and forceful, more forceful than he'd ever been. They grew lost in one another until they both climaxed. Afterwards, they caught their breath. Neither said a word. It was unspoken; they would rest and make love again. They would do this until dawn.

With sunrise peeking through the opening in the curtain, they lay on their sides, his arms wrapped around her waist, spooning her. Their eyes closed. She loved being held by Jesse this way and fell asleep quickly. He remained awake. He nestled his head against hers. It had been a perfect night of love-making. But then something spoiled it. Harmony talked in her sleep. She said one word, "Peter."

Jesse opened his eyes.

Chapter 7

Detective Guerrero arrived at the station at five o'clock Monday morning with a Del Taco breakfast burrito and a cup of coffee in hand. He'd only gotten about three hours of sleep because his mind continuously chewed on what-ifs surrounding the Archibald Bent murder. He sat down, bid good morning to the five ladies in the two framed photographs he kept on his desk, and turned on the computer. As it fired up, he wriggled out of his suit jacket, twisted round and hung it on the back of his chair. Then he sipped his caffeine and took a bite of flour tortilla, sausage, egg, and cheese. Most mornings he ate at home. But the Archibald Bent murder—and he was convinced it was murder, not some weird accident—intrigued him and he wanted to get going.

He didn't have a cleaned-up version of the camera footage yet. Hopefully he would soon, and it would reveal more than what he saw in the grainy copy. He had watched it a few times before going home with the notion that his subconscious might come up with some ideas about what it meant. One inspirational thought did rise to the top. The murder had something to do with Andrea, also known as Double A—huge rock star, ex-con, arsonist, and murderer. He had the big picture about who she was, but that was it. He needed to do a lot more research. He thought the rants Archibald unleashed on his website about her could have inspired bad behavior by some overzealous fan. Some very bad behavior, indeed. But could it have inspired murder? The answer in a nutshell was yes. Detective Guerrero had worked hundreds of cases and knew human beings committed murder for the paltriest of reasons. "He looked at me wrong." "They were laughing and I knew it was about me." "She kept parking in my parking spot. I couldn't take it anymore." "I just felt like it, that's all. I didn't know the guy."

Guerrero signed in to a law enforcement database that would reveal all of Andrea Ashton's brushes with the law. Surprisingly, she did not have much of a rap sheet. Her troubles began after she'd become a worldwide sensation—after she'd met that boyfriend of hers. Indictments and convictions included aiding and abetting in the disposal of a corpse, tampering with evidence, giving false statements to the police, accomplice to murder, and helping a fugitive escape justice. She copped a plea and served seven years in prison.

The detective dug up transcriptions of her interviews with the police as well as the records of her appearances in court. From what he read, Andrea had fallen in love with a criminal known as Catastrophe. He looked up Catastrophe's records as well. The information on him brought up page after page of criminal charges dating back to his teens. The guy was bad news. Guerrero doubted Andrea knew what she was getting into when she started stepping out with him.

Catastrophe had killed before. Once he'd gotten off when a witness recanted. Once he'd served ten years for involuntary manslaughter. In the case involving Andrea, he'd started seeing an ex-girlfriend named Naomi while he still claimed to be in love with Andrea. Guerrero doubted this criminal knew the meaning of love. He was an obvious sociopath who saw the platinum-selling singer as a golden opportunity to get rich. Plans derailed when Naomi grew possessive and jealous. She started making threats, at least in his first version of the story. According to Catastrophe, he accidentally killed Naomi trying to stop her from murdering Andrea. He was a good guy, a hero, for saving Andrea's life. The problem was, he shot Naomi ten times with a Glock 19 he wasn't supposed to have in his possession. There was nothing accidental about ten shots that didn't miss their mark, including one bullet that penetrated right between the eyes. When the police pointed out that what he claimed was contrary to the evidence, Catastrophe changed his story. Andrea had shot and killed Naomi because she'd found out about them and she was jealous. He'd help *her* cover up the crime, not the other way around.

Guerrero shook his head. Some of these guys were simply stupid. Catastrophe expected the police to believe Andrea had killed Naomi from the stage at the Hollywood Bowl where she was performing? And Andrea, who had never handled a gun in her life, had the skill to pop someone right between the eyes?

Guerrero stopped reading and rubbed his forehead. He glanced at his watch. Ten thirty. He'd been reviewing documents and reading transcripts for hours. He'd been so engrossed, he hadn't even grabbed a cup of station coffee from the break room. Sully would have brewed a pot by now—probably a third pot, come to think of it. The department employees did love their dark roast.

Carrying his personal mug embossed with "World's Best Granddad", he lumbered through the station abuzz with ringing phones, clacking computer keys, and police banter. Most of the personnel preferred funny quotes on their mugs such as, "My job is to protect your ass, not kiss it." Or "Hate cops? Next time you have a problem call a crack head." Guerrero was partial to the embrace of family and liked his mug's saying best, even though it had clearly been broken in two and glued back together. His daughter had given it to him when his only grandchild had been born.

He entered the break room. A fresh pot was ready for the pouring, the gurgling about to stop.

Good ol' Sully.

Guerrero poured the brew into his mug and left it black. Leaning against the counter, he savored a sip.

Ahhh. That'll get the old gray cells alert and motorized.

Detective Berry poked his head in. "Hey, Donato. That electronics kid is here to give his statement. I put him in interrogation B. I assume you want to take it rather than me."

"I do have some questions." With lips against the rim of the mug, he shuffled out.

When he entered the interview room, he saw Jordan sitting away from the table, ankle on knee, foot wagging like the tail of an excited collie.

"Nervous?" the detective asked as he sat across from the young man.

"Nope. Nope. Just have extra energy. Always do. Curse of youth, I suspect. Don't suppose you remember those days, huh, Padre?"

"Oh, you'd be surprised what I remember." He tossed a pen and pad of lined paper at Jordan. "Now let's see what you remember about Saturday night. Write it all down. Don't miss a beat. Even if you don't think it's important."

"Will do, sir!" Jordan scooped up the pen and began to write. Guerrero watched the wiz kid with an analytical eye.

Detective Berry entered and gave the table a tap. "That cleaned-up video is ready. You can access it on your computer."

Jordan looked up from the pad of paper. "You have a cleaned-up video of Archie? You could clean it up?" He grinned from ear to ear.

"You don't miss a trick, do you?" Berry stepped back.

Guerrero tried to ask his fellow detective a question. "Hey, did you take a look—?"

Berry was out, closing the door. Guerrero decided the gringo had left the building long ago, so to speak. He took a ginger chew from a bag in his pocket and popped it into his mouth. Ginger helped soothe his stomach when people got under his skin.

"Can I watch it?" Jordan asked.

"The Bent video? Why would you ask that?"

"I'd like to see what happened."

"Well, do you mind if the police go over it first?"

"Oh. Yeah. Sure. What was I thinking?" Jordan smacked the side of his head with his palm, then returned to his statement.

He was a funny kid. Guerrero wondered if he had anything to do with what happened. Aside from designing the murder weapon, that was. He did have an alibi. Remy had confirmed he was with her. But how could a wizard with electronics like this kid set up faulty cameras? It didn't make sense.

Jordan finished and tossed down the pen. "There you go."

"I have a question for you, Jordan," the detective said.

"Yeah?"

"You installed the cameras, correct?"

"Yeah."

"Four of 'em."

"Yeah."

"Well, it's clear you're good at what you do. Why wouldn't three of those cameras work?"

"They didn't work?" Jordan looked amazed.

"Nope. *Nada*. They didn't record."

"Uh, I don't understand. I tested them. Sabotage maybe?" Jordan looked perplexed. Overly perplexed, Guerrero thought.

"And can you think of anyone who would want to do that?" Guerrero asked.

"The killer?"

"You've changed your mind? Now you think there was a killer?"

"I don't know. Maybe. You know what they're saying online, don't ya?"

"Enlighten me."

"The ghost of Andrea did it. Because of all those things Archie posted on his blog."

Guerrero suppressed a groan. "Let's skip the fairy tale, okay? Do you have any thoughts on who the killer might be, aside from Andrea the ghost?"

"How would I know?" Jordan gave an exaggerated expression of disbelief.

There he goes again, Guerrero thought. *Overstated reaction.*

"I told you," Jordan said. "Archie was cool. I don't know why anyone would want him dead."

"Well, here's another thing. The only camera that worked wasn't aimed at the guillotine. All three of the others seemed to be lined up so that they would have recorded it, had they worked. Any thoughts on that?"

"Not really." He shrugged a couple of times. "I mean, they all should have recorded."

Guerrero nodded, unconvinced. Jordan was no slouch. Non-working cameras? It was odd. Especially since the camera that did record didn't show anyone but Archibald entering the room before he was killed. Guerrero had already learned that Jordan's prints were the only ones found on the cameras. So unless they were messed with remotely by someone else . . .

"Nah," Guerrero said aloud.

"Nah, what?" Jordan asked.

"Why shut down three and not all four?"

Jordan offered an inflated shrug of innocence.

"Okay. I guess that's all." Guerrero stared at Jordan, thoughts continuing. He'd like to have the lab take a look at Jordan's phone, but if he asked him for it, that would give the kid a heads-up. It was better to get a court order first and ambush him.

"Is there something else?" Jordan asked, reacting to the detective's probing stare.

"No. You can go. Have Detective Berry walk you out."

Jordan hopped out of the chair. "Okay, sweet. Bye, Padre." He high-tailed it out of there.

Guerrero traipsed back to his desk and grabbed the phone. He punched in an extension. "Hey. Get me a court order to confiscate Jordan Lyman's phone and to obtain records from his carrier. We also need authorization to seize his computer." The cop listened. "Lyman made the murder weapon. He found the body. He did all the electronics. That should be enough for a judge. We specifically need to know who the kid was in contact with and if he built a second remote."

Guerrero hung up. He clicked a link on his computer that would allow him to connect to the cleaned-up version of Archibald Bent's murder and watched. He watched it twice before he checked to be sure he could access the video on his iPad. Then he grabbed his coat and headed for Archibald's house. He wanted to walk through the murder on site with the video as his guide.

Chapter 8

The sunlight streaming through Harmony's window helped wake her at noon. She stretched, yawned and looked to the left side of the bed. Jesse was gone. He'd sneaked out without saying goodbye. She would have thought it considerate of him to allow her to sleep except for the fact that he didn't know she had no Monday morning clients. She dismissed the thought. It wasn't his job to make certain she was conscientious.

She slid her feet into the soft slippers with the dragonfly motif on the floor beside the bed, then shuffled to the bathroom. Before she took a shower, she checked for messages on her phone. There were a few, mostly appointment reminders for the week, and one text from Jesse: "I'll always remember last night." She nodded. She would, too.

There were no messages from Peter which was what she really wanted to see. For an instant she thought about calling him. She was so afraid something bad had happened. She prayed those suicidal tendencies she'd seen when they first met were not making a comeback. But she'd already left one message urging him to call her office and it wouldn't be proper to pester him. She expelled a deep breath. She wouldn't call. It was up to him to contact her.

***

Pete lay in bed in the master suite of his enormous, opulent mansion, eyes on his cell phone resting on the nightstand. He felt the urge to call Dr. McKenna but refused to do so. Andrea didn't want him to see her and he was afraid to cross his sister. Peter wasn't certain what a ghost like Andrea was capable of, and he didn't want to find out. He didn't want her to hurt anyone.

His life was in shambles, and he couldn't understand why. Everything that happened to ruin him had been something out of his control—Andrea and her moment of insanity, strangers attacking his reputation, countless lies people took as gospel. It was crazy.

He thought about Andrea and how close they'd been growing up. Their parents were jet-setting record executives who hobnobbed with political types and earned obscene amounts of money. They were rarely home for long stretches of time. The mansion Pete lived in had been theirs. He and Andrea inherited it after they died in a plane crash.

A plane crash, a twist of fate, had stolen his parents' life of privilege.

A deadly nightclub fire courtesy of his sister had stolen Pete's.

The mansion was way too large for one person. It had been built with a master suite, living room, ballroom, study, office, kitchen, dining room, and guest suite on the first floor. On the second floor there were four additional guest suites, a movie room, a second office, and library. There were twelve bathrooms in all. While Pete had taken up residence in the master suite on the first floor, Andrea had claimed the guest suite on the second floor at the end of a hall, as far away from Pete's bedroom as the house allowed. Not because they were estranged, because they weren't. It just made sense. It gave them both the most privacy possible.

Pete felt a gentle hand on his shoulder, and then heard Robina's kind voice.

"You are supposed to meet with Wayne."

He groaned. "Oh, cancel it. I don't want to go anywhere today."

"He wants to show you his plans for rebuilding the club."

Pete flopped onto his back and rubbed his eyes. "I know. But . . ." His mouth was dry. He licked his lips.

"And you need to eat something."

"I'm not hungry." Pete threw his legs over the side of the bed and sat, head in hands. He sighed. "I'm so tired."

"Eat. Take your vitamins. Drink some water."

Pete stroked the scratchy stubble on his jaw. "It's Wayne. He won't care what I wear. But I better shave."

***

Pete gazed at the ham sandwich and glass of beer sitting in front of him on the desk. He would have felt like he was five years old if the beer had been milk. He didn't like milk. He had never liked milk and was glad it was beer. Although he hadn't drunk beer in years and he wouldn't drink it from this glass either.

"You've cut your hair. You've gained some weight. That shrink you're seeing must be doing you some good." Wayne pointed at the sandwich and beer. "But just in case." Pete's long-time business partner leaned back in his chair, his two hundred and ten pounds making it creak. Ice-blue eyes drilled into Pete, checking for signs of wear, tear, and mental stability. Both of them were a couple of years shy of forty. Wayne had always looked older, partly because he rarely smiled.

Pete stared at the alcohol. "What kind of beer is that?"

"What difference does it make? It's calories."

"Is it your brand?"

"Are you picky about beer now?"

"I saw this article online. If you drink Coors Light, you're one thing. If you drink Bud Light you're another. If you drink something else you could be a serial killer. No, that wasn't it. You cheat on girlfriends and they should run for the hills."

That got a smile out of Wayne and he even chuckled. It was sort of a running joke between them, Pete trying to make Wayne smile.

"Well. I suppose making jokes is a good sign. You've regained your sense of humor." Wayne leaned forward, the smile now gone.

Pete looked at the food with absolutely no appetite. He reached for the sandwich and took a small bite. Wayne was a loyal friend, not just a business partner. When the hits kept coming as a result of the fire, Wayne stuck by him.

"All right. Let's jump right in. It's been five years. Lawsuits are behind us. Well, except for that one. But I'm not worried about it. The guy's reaching for pie in the sky. He wasn't even in the club. I've battled with the insurance company about how much they owe to cover our losses and they've finally agreed to a number I'm satisfied with."

"They quit saying we're partly to blame?"

"Our lawyers wore them down and threatened to sue. We were cleared by the police. We ran that club by the book. We kept excellent records and they owe what they owe. It's that cut and dried. They don't want to go to court over it. That would just cost them, and they know they'd lose in the end."

Pete nodded. He held the sandwich but didn't eat.

"So I say it's time to move forward. While you've been getting your shit together, meaning your head, I've made some decisions I want to run by you."

"Okay."

"We need to rebuild and I don't want to move locations. We'll change the layout of the place. Looks, décor, the whole enchilada. I think we should build a parking structure so we can increase the square footage of the building." He pulled a sheet of paper to the middle of the desk. "This is a rough sketch of what I'm thinking. It's just preliminary. I've contacted an architect. Haven't hired anybody. I just wanted to talk costs, time. Get an idea, you know?"

Pete felt his heart begin to race. He wasn't sure he could do this. He didn't know if he could run a nightclub again. Not after what happened. The vision of being inside the building as it burned came back to him. The smoke. The screams. The cries for help. The patrons lying dead outside the building. The experience had been terrifying. He was terrified now. He started to hyperventilate. Sweat ran into his eyes and he wiped it away.

Wayne reached for the phone. "I'll call 911."

Pete vehemently shook his head. "Just give me a minute." He grabbed hold of the desk to stop the spinning sensation.

Wayne put the phone down. "All right. Clearly I'm laying this on you too soon. I thought, ah, from the last time we talked, that you were doing better."

"I was." Pete's breathing grew more regular, but he was close to tears. "She's come back."

"You're seeing Andrea again?"

Pete looked into Wayne's eyes and held his breath. He knew Wayne thought Andrea's ghost was a hallucination. He exhaled. "I'm sorry."

"No need to be. You were there that night. I wasn't. Makes a difference." Wayne moved the sketch aside. "We can talk about this another time."

"I was thinking. I might never be able to function the way I used to and if that's the case, then I'm nothing but a burden. It's not fair to you if—"

Wayne waved him off. "Don't even go there. You will get better. You *are* getting better. You found the right shrink."

"I thought I had."

"Had? What happened?"

"Andrea doesn't want me to see her."

"Hmm. What does Robina think? Is she still around?"

"She's my rock."

Wayne sucked on the inside of one cheek. He leaned back in the creaky chair. "Here's a thought. I could make decisions for the both of us and that way we can get this project off the ground. You just have to trust me enough. I'll keep you informed of every important decision, of course."

Pete stared into the beer and barely nodded.

Wayne wove his fingers together and cracked his knuckles. "I don't know how much you pay attention to social media. Or if you've been thinking about it. But it's the five-year anniversary of the fire. And to put a cherry on top of the sundae, they discovered some music of your sister's that had never been released and they released it. So Andrea is all over the news and it's stirring up everything. Some marketing firm is having an orgasmic heyday raking in the dough."

"Yeah," Pete mumbled. "I try not to see it. But it's tough to avoid."

"I know. It's hard to believe how many loons there are claiming she isn't really dead."

Pete raised his line of sight. "Or claiming she's a ghost."

"I didn't say that. But yeah. Aside from you, there are those who claim that, too. "

Pete rose to his feet. "You have my permission to do as you see fit. Whatever you want. Heaven knows I'm in no condition to decide anything."

He walked out, leaving behind the sandwich with the single bite taken from it and the untouched beer.

***

Detective Guerrero's coat hung on the back of his chair. His shirt sleeves were rolled up, and his hands were clasped behind his head. He'd returned from the Bent mansion more determined than ever to understand what happened. He stared at the computer monitor on his desk and let out a long, low groan just as a female detective clacked by on stylish, but impractical, red high heels.

"How many times you gonna watch that, Donato?" the young detective asked. She was impeccably groomed, her white blouse and blue pencil skirt neatly pressed, her dark hair pulled into a tight bun.

"As long as it takes, Detective Hernandez. Or until my retirement date rolls around." He grunted and lowered his arms. "Don't those shoes hurt your feet?"

"I'm breaking them in. Big date. I've got some flats under my desk." She nodded at his computer. "Care for another set of eyes?"

He motioned at the screen. "Be my guest."

He started to get up so she could sit down, but she put up her manicured hands with the long, red-polished nails. "That's okay." She bent down and took a look over his shoulder. "This is that rich guy who lost his head, right?"

"That's one way of putting it." He clicked so the video would play.

The two detectives watched Archibald turn on the lights as he stepped into the Great Room. He paused, savoring his creation before he began to wander about looking at the wax figures. If he stayed to the middle of the room, he was caught on camera. When he strayed too far left, right or forward, he disappeared from sight. The lab had done a good job of clarifying the video. It wasn't perfect, but it wasn't the grainy mess it had been before.

They watched Archibald react to something unpleasant and begin to cough while covering his nose.

"He smells something bad," Detective Hernandez commented. "Did the techs find the source of it?"

"No. Nothing."

Archibald reacted to the sound of the entrance doors slamming shut, only one seen on camera. Guerrero paused the video. "Sometimes we get sound and sometimes we don't. It's a fluke of some kind. Disappointing. After watching this, I went back to the house and tried to match what-was-what with the video. Except for the mannequin of Marie Antoinette remaining a burnt-up mess, things looked in order."

He clicked Play and they continued to review.

"Now he's locked in," Guerrero said. "He calls out, but we can't hear. Then suddenly this music blares."

"Double A. That's Double A," Detective Hernandez said excitedly. "You may not have heard of her, but she was a big deal for a while. Some new music she made a long time ago was recently found and her label just released it. That music is hers. It could be important, and I bet you didn't know that."

"Except I have a teenage granddaughter who comes to my house and she likes to share with her old Papa. Sometimes she makes me feel young. You know, because I learn about young people and what they like, including the music of Double A. But mostly I feel like a relic."

"Aww," responded Detective Hernandez.

"Okay, now this tells us no one was working the remote, because he finds it on the snack table. The whiz kid who set this up swears he only made one remote. If there is a second one, a lot of this can be explained away."

"He's coughing. He looks scared," Hernandez said. "We see him then we don't. He comes back into frame. He's talking. Oh, the sound cut out." She frowned.

"I had a lip reader take a look. He's saying 'That's impossible. Why don't you move when I'm watching?' And then we can hear him shouting because the sound comes back."

"Weird."

"The whole thing's weird. Okay, here he's in the center of the room and something drips on his hand. We know from Jordan that it's fake blood àla *House on Haunted Hill*."

"Okay. I've seen that."

"But the lab analyzed it. Concentrated sulfuric acid, not harmless fake red blood. And he reacts like it burned him. And he drops the remote and loses it."

"Were there burns on his hand?"

"I'll get the report soon. Okay, now he's out of view. I don't know what's going on. I assume he's near the guillotine. Joan of Arc's pyre flares. Marie Antoinette starts to burn. Since Archibald lost the remote, we know he didn't turn them on. He comes back into view and rushes to the burning mannequin. There's nothing he can do. He rushes out of frame. And ... we hear him struggling and calling out for someone to stop." Archibald's scream sounded. Guerrero and Hernandez flinched.

Hernandez reached in and paused the player. "You've watched the video to see what happened before Archie entered the room? No one came in?"

"Not through the door we see on camera. And if he or she entered through the other door, that person never came into view of the camera."

He clicked Play. A woman's laugh is heard on the recording.

"Oh, my God," Hernandez halfway whispered.

Guerrero paused the video again. "What?"

He looked at her and saw she'd gone pale.

"What?" he asked again.

She looked at Guerrero with questioning eyes. "Um. Let it play."

He started the video. Off screen Archibald is heard screaming hysterically, "Please! Please! Oh, please."

A woman's voice says: "There's nothing I could do."

Then came the swoosh of the falling blade. A loud chop. And a dull thud.

Guerrero stopped the video. "If I fast forward we'll see Jordan and Remy arriving together." He stared at the screen. "So what do you think?"

He looked at Hernandez. She was staring silently at the screen. "Are you all right?" he asked.

Her lips moved and finally she spoke. "That laugh. That voice. That's Double A. I've heard her a million times on talk shows, podcasts and stuff."

"She's dead."

"I know. But that's her. Do a voice comparison. You'll see. You'll see I'm right."

"What are you saying?" Guerrero asked.

"Just what legions of fans will say. That she came back and killed this guy. For years there've been rumors. Andrea's a ghost. Andrea didn't start that fire, her brother did. She's out for revenge."

"Then why kill this guy instead of her brother?" Guerrero shook his head.

"Didn't he insult her on a bunch of website posts?"

"You've been checking on the case."

"Everyone's talking about it."

"Everyone except Detective Berry." He looked to the ceiling and back. "Okay, one vote for 'the ghost did it.' Thanks for your help." He scooted closer to the desk.

She moved to the side of his chair. "I didn't say I believe that. I am a cop. I'm just saying, that was her laugh. That was her voice. This video sure makes it look like something supernatural."

He turned in his chair and faced her. "There's no such thing as ghosts. In fact, I'd hazard a guess there isn't even life after death. When you die, that's it. You're worm fodder."

Hernandez' eyes shifted to the photographs on Guerrero's desk. She spoke gently. "Your wife and kids. They were killed by a drunk driver, right? Wouldn't it help to believe in something and not be so cynical?"

"Excuse me," Guerrero said.

"Sorry. I know you never talk about them. But maybe you should."

"Hernandez . . ."

She stepped back. "I'm just saying sometimes it helps. And how many years has it been since they died?"

Guerrero's stomach churned. He felt like yelling at her. He felt like telling her she was out of line, insubordinate, a terrible person, even though in his heart of hearts he was fully aware she meant well. He held his tongue.

"Okay. I'll leave you with this," Hernandez said. "Be prepared because I promise you, and I won't be the one doing it, but that video is going to get leaked. Mark my words." She clacked off in her heels.

Guerrero took out a ginger chew and chewed.

Chapter 9

Jesse owned four vehicles. A Dodge Challenger Demon with all the bells and whistles, meant to impress with sinister speed; a Mercedes E350 for elegance and class; a Chevy Colorado truck, good for the property he owned in a remote location in Lucerne Valley; and a Volkswagen bug, tan in color, his inside joke and homage to someone he admired. He only drove it on special occasions. Harmony didn't even know he owned it.

Jesse sat in his Volkswagen at the curb two doors down from Pete's massive mansion in Bel Air and eagle-eyed the street as if he were a cop on stakeout. He'd done this before, after Harmony had talked about Pete in her sleep once too often. She always referred to him as Peter, not Pete as everyone else called him. It caused Jesse to feel a deep-seated need to tail the guy. He could agree that Pete would have been a great catch five years ago, before his life literally went up in smoke, but not now. He looked like a starving vagrant who had found expensive clothes and managed to stay clean. Yes, he still had a hefty bank account in order to maintain the ritzy house and car, but—Jesse mused—all that could change in an instant, especially if someone helped.

A white BMW approached, the third one he'd seen, but this one slowed, allowing for a wide gate to slide open and provide access to a driveway. Jesse slid down in the seat and watched Pete pull onto his property, then stop. Jesse lifted a pair of binoculars. He saw Pete talking to someone in the passenger seat. He also saw that no one was there.

Jesse snorted with satisfaction. "Yeah, this guy's two donuts short of a dozen. Harmony, Harmony, Harmony. You sure know how to pick 'em."

The conversation with no one lasted for about three minutes. Then Pete backed the car out, the gate began to close, and he drove right past the Volkswagen. Jesse turned the starter and made a u-turn. He followed Pete for thirty-five minutes to the city of North Hollywood, or Noho, as it was known.

Pete parked his BMW smack-dab in front of a well-groomed apartment building that looked as if it had been built in the sixties. It was one of those horseshoe-configuration jobbies with two sets of stairs, one on each end of the shoe, twelve apartments in all. A "For Rent" sign was neatly displayed in front.

Jesse pulled to the curb across the street, behind a couple of cars, and watched Pete climb the stairs on the left. He knocked on the door of the end apartment and stood stone-still as he waited for someone to answer. The apartment's living room window faced a courtyard where tall plants and trees provided a modicum of privacy. Jesse wouldn't be able to see who opened the door from his viewpoint and he decided it wouldn't be prudent to get closer on foot. He'd be an obvious stalker to anyone paying attention. All he needed was the apartment number anyway, and he could probably find out who lived at this address on Riverton if he ever had reason to.

As Pete waited for someone to answer, something strange occurred. A man who looked to be in his thirties with long dark hair and a full beard unexpectedly pushed aside the blinds of the window that faced the street and locked eyes with Jesse. A startling and unpleasant sensation shot through his chest, almost as if he'd been harpooned with an arrow. Who was this guy? What made him look outside now? And why was he staring at him? Jesse refused to turn away. He never allowed anyone to intimidate him, if indeed, that was what this person was trying to do. There was no malice in the person's face, just a countenance of curiosity, as if he knew Jesse had followed Pete.

The man released the blinds and a few seconds later, Pete was allowed in the door. Jesse decided it was time to head out. Who knew how long Pete would be in the apartment, and he'd learned what he really wanted to know. Harmony was not with her dream lover.

Jesse took the time to figure out his next move and decided to make a run to his apartment in Sherman Oaks for a few things before leaving town. He needed to think, to regroup. He needed time away from the crowded city and his confusing relationship with Harmony. He needed to sort out his emotions and decide who he was and what he wanted.

***

Darius put his hands together prayerfully and gave a little bow. "*Namaste*," he said.

"*Namaste*," Pete said in return.

Darius swept an outstretched arm toward the beanbag lounger.

Pete swallowed and sat down. The beans rustled under his weight, sounding much like the crunching of dried leaves. "I know I was just here... I had a panic attack. I thought maybe another prayer. Some meditation."

"Certainly." Darius sat on the floor and crossed his legs. "Have you been doing meditation at home?"

Pete looked uncomfortable. "No," he confessed. "I tried. I don't do it right."

"Well. Practice makes progress, not perfection. You should get Robina to help you."

"I should." He paused. "I will," he promised, wondering how Darius knew Robina's name. He'd never introduced her. But then, Darius was a psychic medium, supposedly.

Darius rested his hands palms-up on his knees and closed his eyes. He didn't say anything. Pete watched for a while and wondered why the medium didn't start the instructions to breathe in, breathe out. Picture a meadow. Relax.

They remained in the silence for ten minutes, only Pete couldn't unwind. He kept wondering why Darius was doing things differently.

"Hmmm," Darius finally said. "She wants me to tell you it's too late."

"Who? What?"

"Harmony needs to watch out."

"She—the ghost—wants to hurt Dr. McKenna?" Pete asked.

"I don't think so." Darius answered.

"I don't understand."

"Andrea says she was warning you away, but it's too late. The two of you became too close. Watch out. That's all I can tell you."

Pete felt his heart start to launch and he began to breathe too quickly. Darius stood up with no effort at all, walked to Pete, and placed his hands on Pete's shoulders. Instantly Pete felt a calming energy soothe his body, mind, and soul.

***

Jesse drove north on Interstate 15 toward his sixty-acre spread tucked away in a remote corner of Lucerne Valley. It was his personal getaway destination, a place he'd christened Scarlett because of the blood-red sunset he'd experienced the first night he stayed. He visited at least once a month, usually for the weekend. This time, however, he would remain for an extended stay while he got his act together. The twenty-five-hundred-square-foot ranch house he'd built made that easy. For years he'd allowed the place to sit without a caretaker, relying on barbed-wire fences for security as well as a gate with a security code. All it took was one time discovering vandals had damaged the house for Jesse to take action.

He reconfigured a barn into a livable space and hired a man who owned an intimidating Chow mix called Fluffy, of all names, to take up residence.

"Afternoon." Hawkeye nodded, Fluffy by his side barking his brains out at Jesse seated in the Volkswagen bug. "Shut it," the caretaker commanded, and the big dog closed his yap. "How ya' doin'?" Hawkeye started again. He was the friendly sort, a man in his late forties, lean and fit. He favored red plaid flannel shirts in the winter and blue, patterned, short-sleeve, button-front shirts in the summer. He always wore jeans and a cowboy hat.

"Well, I'll tell you," Jesse answered now that it was quiet enough to hear. "That's what I plan to figure out. Would you open the garage for me?"

"Sure thing."

The automatic door opener had quit working and a replacement part had yet to arrive.

Jesse rolled into the four-car garage and parked on the far-left side, the Chevy Colorado that stayed at Scarlett just to the right. He headed for the house with a small carryall in hand. Hawkeye matched his stride as he rambled on with a report about how things had been since Jesse's last visit, including something about a neighbor and a propane tank. Jesse hardly listened. He wanted a shower and a place to think. He entered the house and closed the door on Hawkeye mid-sentence.

That evening Jesse sat in a recliner, a glass of Wild Turkey in one hand, and gazed at the mantle of stars seen through the large living room window. It was as if God had thrown a bucket of radiant diamonds across the heavens just for him. The occasional howl of a coyote and the whisper of a gentle wind kept the world from being completely silent and still.

Six years ago Harmony had entered his life and made him a better man. She didn't know it, but he used to come into her hospital room and watch her sleep—just watch as she breathed in and out, her chest gently rising and falling in perfect rhythm. The large bandage on the left side of her face hid the result of a gruesome act that had been performed on her only days earlier. She mesmerized him and he didn't understand why. She was just a pretty young woman like any other pretty young woman, but she'd survived something horrendous, and from what he'd observed once he'd made his move and started talking to her, she didn't complain. That elevated her in his eyes. As he spent more and more time with her, and came to know her, she became important to him.

Soon they found themselves talking every day, and when she went home, he played nursemaid. Not in an overbearing way, just enough to help her heal. Perhaps more importantly, he listened to her talk about how she felt about the attack. How she felt about the scars, especially the one on her face that would draw the attention of everyone who caught a glimpse.

"I don't care," she would say. "Well, I do care, but it doesn't matter. It happened. I can't change it. I refuse to live my life in fear. Time to move on."

Jesse wasn't a time-to-move-on type of guy. He held grudges. He'd been born with the proverbial silver spoon in his mouth and was given the best of everything. Well, almost the best. It seemed to him his older brother got a little bit better. A little bit more attention. A little bit more love. Once his brother had been given twelve Christmas presents while Jesse had only received eleven. "They cost the same," his mother explained. Jesse didn't care. He was ten. He didn't understand the concept. The next day he sneaked into his brother's room and destroyed half of his haul. Jesse'd received a spanking, the only spanking of his life, but it was worth it to him because he'd gotten even.

As a kid, Jesse considered himself the best athlete in his grammar school because of his size and strength. Despite that, he wasn't tapped first when it came to picking teams. The first time it happened he squawked, but let it pass. The second time he beat the kid up after school. He was never chosen second after that.

Jesse considered this behavior normal. Who didn't want the best? Who didn't want to be first pick? Most kids weren't willing to do something about it, but he was. Adults took revenge, too. At least his mother did. When Jesse was thirteen he caught her putting ex-lax in a batch of brownies. "Your father," she explained, "is having an affair. I'm letting him know how shitty I think that is." She laughed. "Shitty. Get it?"

Jesse didn't get it. But he did get that it was okay to get people back.

The thing was, when he committed his first murder at the age of fourteen, he wasn't getting someone back. He was after a thrill. He strangled a six-year-old girl, a neighbor and the daughter of one of his mother's friends, after he spotted her riding her bike alone in the street. Leopold and Loeb had nothing on him. He did what he did for the same reason they did what they did. For fun. Only Jesse got away with it, and his list of offenses grew.

Jesse maintained a journal of the crimes he committed, and hid it on the highest shelf in the left corner of his bedroom closet. At first he feared that if his mother discovered it, he'd have to kill her. But then he realized she never cleaned the house, a house cleaner did, and Jesse didn't allow the cleaner in his room. He considered his journal and his mother safe.

By the age of eighteen Jesse had murdered four times and he knew what his major and minor would be in college: psychology and sociology. How else would he ever understand what made him tick? As it turned out he never understood. Sure, he sought revenge the times he felt jealous, but what about the people he hurt who did nothing? He had no explanation for that and apparently neither did the books he read. From what he discerned, he could be labeled a psychopath, and he kind of liked it. He was the way he was. He was of the opinion psychopaths couldn't be cured, so why even fight it? He was good with people. He could make them feel at ease. He could make them think that he was concerned with their feelings and problems. He could lure anyone into a sense of safety and then demolish their trust in an instant. He considered it a talent.

In the case of Harmony, he did care. Not at first. After all, he was the complete stranger who had knifed her. He'd wanted to see if he could pull off an attack in public in broad daylight. He'd disfigured her, given her ugly scars that would forever be a reminder of what happened. He didn't go to the hospital to finish her off, which is what one might expect according to television shows. No, he'd gone out of inquisitiveness. He thought of it as research for his line of work as a psychologist. He wanted to know how she'd cope with what he did. He fed her a line of bull about having gone to visit a friend. Then he went to work getting to know her.

He didn't know the exact moment he decided he would no longer kill. He just came to realize that he no longer fantasized about watching the life fade from someone's eyes. Nor did he desire the supreme orgasmic high that would rush through his body by terrorizing some deceived dolt, hacking him to death. Instead, his mind was filled with thoughts of Harmony. He thought about being a regular everyday Joe. He put away his killing kit and for most of the last six years led a conventional life.

His cell phone rang and he grabbed it from the coffee table. *Harmony.* She hadn't phoned all day. She'd texted once and he hadn't responded.

"Hello, my love," he said, his voice full of affection, the expression on his face flat.

"Hi. I haven't heard from you. What's going on?"

"Nothing much. Had a case to review. Needed to come up with some strategies."

"Ah. A psychologist's life is never done. Will you be coming over tonight?"

"I don't think I can."

"Really?"

He stood up and downed the rest of his drink. He gazed into the cut crystal glass. "No, I can't. I'd love to, but..." He sighed. "Harmony, you know how much I adore you."

"Uh oh. That's a bad way to begin a sentence."

"I need to be straight, okay? So just listen. Your relationship with Pete has gotten under my skin."

"He's a client. Was a client."

"I'm aware. But I believe you've crossed an emotional line. How am I supposed to compete with someone who has so consumed you that you dream about him?"

"Jesse. You're the one I love."

Love. Humans threw that word around as a cure-all to every ill. It annoyed him. His eyes narrowed. "I know. And I love you, too," he said sweetly. "Look. I'm going out of town for a while. Visit some old friends. And before you ask, no, you haven't met them."

"Should I worry?"

"No. No, of course not. There's nothing to worry about. I know you love me, I just need some time."

"Okay. You will stay in touch, though. Right?"

"Of course."

"All right, then. I understand. I do. Love you."

"Love you."

They hung up. Jesse poured himself a second drink, lifted the glass, and stared at the amber liquid. "Love you," he said in a sarcastic whisper. All at once, he pitched the glass across the room and smiled at the broken mess it made on the wall and floor.

"Wouldn't it be lovely if that were someone's head?" he murmured.

He took a warm jacket from the closet. Tomorrow he'd call the local woman he'd hired a couple of months back to come clean the house. Rose. That was her name. He shoved his arms in the jacket, made sure he had his car keys and wallet, and left the house.

He drove the winding road up the mountain to Big Bear, which was about twenty miles from Lucerne Valley. It would be very cool in the resort town this time of night in May. With a population of over 12,000, plus tourists, he thought there might be some action going on. He parked on the street in the area known as The Village and began to roam. Pickings were slim. Gift shops were closed and clientele in the restaurants were thinning out. It wasn't like L.A., with nightlife abuzz all hours. He found himself a seat in a sports bar, nursed a beer and watched people playing pool. One sweet little redhead in some of the tightest jeans he'd ever seen smiled at him from a pool table where she'd just missed a shot. As she held up the pool cue, Jesse could see a very cool black and white tattoo on the back of her right hand. It depicted the upper portion of two skeletons in a loving embrace. He smiled as he gazed at it and then he smiled at her. She waved at him to join her, but he shook his head. He had no plans for anything more than nursing his beer and watching others at play. He wasn't prepared.

Chapter 10

Donato Guerrero looked at the empty bowls and dinner plates on his kitchen table and smiled at his seventeen-year-old granddaughter, Esther. She took after him, with his large frame and extra pounds, which wasn't the ideal in today's society. However, she had a face that could rival Elizabeth Taylor's and rich, dark straight hair that fell all the way to her waist. She was also bubbly and positive and had ten million friends. The two of them had consumed all of the courses he'd made: appetizers, **entrée**, and dessert—and now they were sated and at rest. He was a great cook. Everyone he fed agreed.

Esther started to clear the table.

"No. No, no, no." Donato waved a hand at her. "You are my honored guest."

"I'm your granddaughter, Papa." She carried her dirty dishes to the sink, then returned for his. "That was *excelente*! Especially the mole sauce with chilies. *Muchas gracias*."

"*De nada*. But please, leave the dishes in the sink. I'll load the dishwasher after you leave."

"Okay," she relented and sat down. "So have I filled you in with enough of the skinny on Double A? Do you have more questions aside from the obvious one, do I believe she's a ghost?"

"No. Because I can tell by the way you talk that you do."

"Ghosts are merely our energy in another form," Esther said flat out.

"You're an expert, are you?"

"Just how I think of it. We do live on."

"Let's not have this debate," Donato said.

"No debate. God is real," she stated emphatically. "My mother, my aunties, and Grandmama are with him."

Her grandfather acquiesced. "If believing that makes you feel better, who am I to take it away from you?" That's how they always left it. "But to answer your question, I did want to ask about Pete Ashton, Double A's brother, the guy who owned the nightclub."

"People hate him." Esther straightened in her chair.

"But she's the one who burned the place down," Donato said, not understanding.

"Maybe. Some people say he was after insurance money. Some people say he was jealous of his sister's success and wanted her dead."

"But he was successful, too."

"I know. But he thought she should have stayed in prison longer."

"Is that a fact?"

Esther shrugged. "It's just what people think. She has a lot of fans. They love her. They hate that she's dead and he's not. Maybe that's why people like to say she's come back as a ghost."

"Not because she is one."

"We already talked about that. I say, you can't keep a good rock star down." She chuckled.

"So everything is gossip. Nothing is based on fact."

Esther shrugged.

"There's going to be a memorial at the site of the nightclub Thursday night," Donato said. "It's the five-year anniversary of what happened."

"Yeah. I heard about that."

"Are you going?" he asked.

"Not my thing. I mean I love Double A. I don't believe she set the fire. But, nah."

"I think I will," he informed her, crossing his arms.

"Really? Why? And why are you asking me all these questions?"

"It's all connected somehow. Double A and this murder I'm working on. I need to find the thread that unravels it."

"Oh! The guy who got his head chopped off?" Esther drew a line with her finger across her throat. "The one who made fun of Double A and her music?"

"Murder stories travel fast, the more bizarre the better, eh?"

"Tell me about it." She rested the side of her head on her palm, elbow on table, ready for all the dirt.

"I can't. What you saw on the news is what I can share."

Disappointed, she gave him her best pouty face.

"Sorry, *mija*."

"It's okay. I understand. Are you sure you don't want me to load the dishwasher?"

"No. Go on. Go out with your friends. Have fun."

"I'm going to church."

"You are one strange teenager."

"Thanks!" She beamed.

"Thank you for having dinner with me."

She came from her side of the table, put an arm around his shoulder, and gave him a kiss on the cheek. "*Gracias*. Love you, Papa."

"I love you."

She left the house.

Donato rinsed the dishes, loaded the dishwasher and pressed the button that began the cycle. He wiped off the stove and the kitchen table. He swept the floor and turned out the light. The dishwasher purred.

The hefty detective picked up the remote and sat in his comfy recliner in the den. He turned on the TV, ready for something relaxing. Not the news. Definitely not that. However, that's what he saw, and if he tried to change it, the answer was no. The television stayed stubbornly on the same channel.

"What in the world?" He grew more frustrated with each useless press of the button. He tossed the remote aside and lumbered up to the TV to see if he could change the channel that way. *Nada.* Confounded technology! Maybe he'd just turn it off.

Suddenly the television blared. "Channel 7 news has obtained a very interesting video of a strange, mysterious, and brutal murder. While it isn't graphic, it is disturbing when you know what takes place off camera. Viewer discretion is advised."

The detective couldn't believe his eyes. There was his evidence on display for anyone and everyone to see. Hernandez was right. This was the sort of juicy thing news people would pay to get their hands on and did. Someone's head was going to roll.

Detective Guerrero saw red until he realized his choice of words and groaned. All right. Maybe someone's head wouldn't roll, but they sure as hell weren't going to get away with this.

The video of Archibald's murder went viral. News channels repeatedly aired the footage, commenting on what he'd said about Double A only hours before the murder, inflaming her fans. Social media blew up. The story trended on Twitter and Facebook and every other online source. People began to express their take on what happened and who they thought murdered the deserving jerk, Archibald Bent. Double A went to the top of the list. As far as they were concerned, the ghost did it. Comments ran amok.

After what he said about Double A, this doofus deserved what he got.

Ewww. Double A be mad, sure as shit. Do'na blame er.

You go girl.

No such thing as a ghost. Double A AIN'T dead.

Doc Frankenstein said it best. She's alive. Alive!

Here we go again. Blamin the girl for something she didn't do.

Off with his head!

News hosts, influencers, and podcasters reminded followers that a memorial was being held at the burnt-out site to commemorate the five-year anniversary of the nightclub deaths. Everyone was encouraged to come.

***

Pete awoke in the middle of the night alarmed by the barrage of pings, chimes, and jingle alerts coming from his phone. After wiping the sleep from his eyes, he grabbed it and took a look. Someone had gotten hold of his number and released it to the masses. A slew of hateful texts kept on coming from people he'd never even met. Anxiety suddenly shot through him and he dropped the phone as if it were a scorpion about to strike. Overwhelmed, he scrambled to turn it off and fell back on the bed.

Robina sat up and stroked his shoulder. "You're okay. I'm here."

Pete's chest heaved in and out. His mouth emitted short bursts of air. One of the messages even invited him to the nightclub memorial. Then he "could hear *in person* what people thought of him."

***

Jesse arrived home from Big Bear late. The sight of potential, unsuspecting prey excited him. Whatever magical spell Harmony had unknowingly spun was broken. He'd killed once since that spell had cracked. The opportunity for mayhem had dropped in his lap, too delectable to resist.

The visit to Harmony's house the other night had been an attempt to recapture the magic. He'd thought maybe the spell that kept him from killing would return. But she'd destroyed the fantasy of that ever happening with one word: Peter.

Jesse had bought the Lucerne Valley property for two reasons: its remoteness and an abandoned mine. The mine wasn't big. He'd spent some months carving into it to make it larger for his purposes, and now it was perfect. The opening he obscured with the largest rocks he could move. Once entered, there was a twenty-foot path to a wooden door he'd installed by drilling into the granite face. Behind the door was the space he'd enlarged until it was approximately seven by six feet in size. This was where he kept his trophies.

There was no actual trail to the mine, but he had no trouble finding it, even at night. The oversized LED lanterns he owned illuminated as well as any full moon. If he had one thing to do over again, he would have built his home farther away from the entrance. As things were now, the house was only half a mile from the incline of the mountain where the mine jutted into the side.

Jesse grabbed the key to the wooden door and dropped it in his jacket pocket. He took the sack that contained his latest mementos out of the carryall and left the house. As he walked the half mile to the mine, the brisk air felt exhilarating against his skin and invigorating entering his lungs. The lantern helped him avoid any tarantulas, scorpions or snakes that might be in his way. Tonight the approach was mostly clear, with only the occasional lizard and dwarf tarantula scampering out of his path.

As he neared, the lantern light climbed the rocks and shadows and matrixed into weird, creepy smiles. *Perhaps the mine is happy to see me*, he mused with a chuckle. He was certainly more than happy to visit it. He moved behind the rocks he'd used to camouflage the opening and squeezed inside. When he reached the door, he was pleased to see that nothing had been disturbed. He put the key in the lock and turned. A hearty single-handed shove revealed the opening.

An old steamer trunk he'd purchased years back at an antique store held all his treasures. It sat in the center area, reminiscent of an altar placed in a temple's most sacred space. All it needed was an overhead spotlight. The trunk had no lock and Jesse reverently raised the cover. Holding the lantern high, he peered inside. Excitement energized every pore, every cell, every vein. His temple throbbed with anticipation.

"Hello old friends," he said. "Long time, no see."

He lifted a shoebox from the trunk and sat with it on the dirt floor. Removing the lid, he took out more than fifty photos he'd taken of people he'd slaughtered over the years. Like his idol, Ted Bundy, Jesse's prey of choice was pretty young women with long hair—dark or light tresses, he wasn't picky. He'd killed men from time to time, usually when he hadn't done his homework and broken into the apartment of a female whose boyfriend was spending the night, startling him into action in order to save his own skin.

Jesse could recall the circumstances of every kill. He didn't need the photos because everything was hardwired into his brain. But the photos were fun. Tied-up wrists and ankles. Tortured, terrified facial expressions. Tears running down cheeks. He took after-shots as well. Somehow, though, he preferred the ones where his victims were alive.

After only five minutes of reviewing the photos, he stood up and put the shoebox back. The journals from when he was a teen were in the trunk, but he felt no inclination to read them. There were other boxes, one with his victims' jewelry, one with his victims' underwear. There was even a gun, although he'd never used it. He had perfected the use of knives and how to kill with his bare hands.

Jesse took the sack he'd brought with him. First he removed the hood and gloves from the executioner's ensemble. There were dark spots on both items. He grinned as he held them. It was an added bonus to see that Archibald's blood had spurted and stained the fabric.

He threw back his head and laughed. What a high it had been shoving Archibald onto the guillotine and trapping his neck. He remembered the old man's screams and pleas. Who would have thought that little twerp Jordan was such a demented little genius, able to build such a killing machine?

Jesse placed the hood and gloves inside the trunk and then took the second remote Jordan had built from the sack. He put it in the trunk without fanfare.

Jesse's heart beat a little faster as he looked at a rectangular travel case that was approximately seventeen by eleven by three inches in size. He opened it, exposing four stainless steel knives of varying lengths. He'd used all of them to kill at one time or another, but his favorite was the seven-inch fillet knife. He took it from the slot that held it in place and gazed at the blade that was as sharp as the day he purchased it.

"Did you think I'd abandoned you?" he whispered. "I nearly did."

Engrossed in his killing collection, he didn't hear the footsteps come up from behind. The voice, however, drew his attention in a snap.

"Oh, it's you," Hawkeye said. "I saw the light and thought I'd better check out who was roaming around the place."

Always at Hawkeye's side, Fluffy began to growl. "Shut it," Hawkeye commanded. "He's still not used to you. It's okay, boy."

Jesse's back remained to his caretaker as well as the dog. He had time to put the knives back in the trunk and close shop, and he didn't have to explain himself to an employee. The problem was, Hawkeye now knew about his hiding place and that just wasn't acceptable. He remained in place, strategizing what to do.

"Nice little crypt you've got here," Hawkeye commented.

Crypt. Apt description, Jesse thought. He remained silent, his eyes flickering back and forth, waiting and thinking.

"Okay, well, ah, guess we'll leave you to whatever you're doing out here."

"This might be a good test," Jesse said softly.

"What's that?" Hawkeye asked.

"After all, I'm out of practice," Jesse said, his voice even softer, to draw the caretaker in.

Hawkeye stepped closer. "I still couldn't hear you. What's that?"

"I said, maybe you can help me with something." He needed to make sure Hawkeye was good and near. He held the knife in one hand, prepared to use it.

"Help you? What with?"

When he heard the man come even closer and could sense him breathing down his neck, Jesse whipped around and, as quick as the devil, swiped the blade back and forth across Hawkeye's throat. Blood spurted like the Trevi Fountain. Fluffy started barking and bouncing with every ounce of energy he had.

Hawkeye's hands went to his throat and he dropped to the ground just as Fluffy lunged for Jesse. But Jesse was ready and the knife found its mark. It plunged into the dog's chest and Jesse managed to shove the dog back. It whimpered in pain as it lay in the dirt. Jesse watched Hawkeye and the canine bleed out. When he was sure they were dead, he wiped the knife with a portion of Hawkeye's shirt.

Damn. Now he had to clean things up as well as find a new caretaker, which wasn't as easy as it sounded. Jesse shook his head as he looked at the two carcasses at his feet. Sometimes these things just couldn't be helped, he told himself.

"Sorry, Hawkeye." He sighed. "Didn't really want to do that. But I have to hand it to me. That was pretty good."

A trail ran along the side of the trophy room. It led to a deep pit that Jesse had used in the past on those special times when he needed to dispose of a body. Jesse was pretty certain he could carry the dog, but Hawkeye was a different matter. Dead weight was dead weight, heavy as hell and hard to manage. He'd carried the bodies of some petite young women to the pit without a problem. Hawkeye was bigger and heavier. He'd have to drag him.

Past the room, the path jutted to the left and sloped downward so that gravity would be Jesse's friend. Looping an arm under each of

Hawkeye's armpits and taking hold of the large lantern in his right hand, Jesse began the backward trek, allowing the dead man's feet to drag on the ground. The path was too narrow to use a wheelbarrow or a cart.

"Listen up, friend. If you hadn't been so nosy you wouldn't be in this situation. However, I do recognize that it was your job to look after the property and . . . ." He paused, adjusted his hold on the caretaker, and began again. "You know, I do have to say I'm sorry in your case. I mean, I did hire you to put a stop to trespassers and I can see that was what you were trying to do. The only consolation I can give you is that you'll be spending eternity with Fluffy, and eleven pretty girls. At least they used to be pretty. They're all skeletal by now as I'm a bit out of practice and it's been a while since I dumped anyone down here. If memory serves, the last female I tossed in that pit, was ten years ago. Yeah, about that."

Oh, my god, what a night that was.

Jesse remembered that her name was Connie and she was fifteen. He saw her hitchhiking and picked her up. She was looking to party.

Mmm. Mmm. Sweet, sweet Connie doin' her act, as the song goes.

Connie didn't care if he was in a band, just if he had drugs. Ecstasy was her preference. He had some pot and that was all. She didn't know that when she accepted his invitation to come to his place.

She also liked to drink and dance. She did a very delectable strip tease for him. He didn't even have to ask. He might not have killed her, but after they had sex, she turned into a literal shrew. She ragged on that he had to have ecstasy. She knew he did. "If you want more," she said, "then I need more." She never got her ecstasy, but Jesse did.

He grunted as he raised up to give his back a short rest. "Not as young as I used to be, for sure. Okay, Hawkeye. Almost there."

He walked the last twenty feet, pulling Hawkeye to his desolate resting place in silence. Once he arrived, he dropped the body near the edge and peered over the side. The pit wasn't all that deep, only about fifty feet from where he stood to the top of the rubble. The bodies of previous victims were camouflaged with rocks he'd tossed on them to help lessen any odor that might have attracted scavenging animals. He didn't know if a vulture could find its way into the mine and the pit. A coyote sure could, and judging from the slope of some of the rocks, an animal like that could make its way in and out. Jesse didn't need a coyote prancing around with a human femur in its mouth.

He squinted and thought he could see the protruding finger bones of one of his victims, curled as if grasping for a lifeline. Rocks settling, he thought. It couldn't have been a last-ditch effort to rise out of the rocks. No, he decided. It couldn't be. His victims had all been dead when he tossed them in, of that he was sure.

Jesse kicked Hawkeye unceremoniously over the side and watched him plummet. When the body hit bottom, he heard the sound of a thud, along with the knocking together of disturbed ore. Jesse would gather rocks to cover him after he dropped Fluffy in to join his master.

Chapter 11

Beneath the bright morning sun, Jordan stood outside his mother's detached garage where he lived and stared at the search warrant Detective Guerrero had handed him. A short, thin woman in her fifties pulled on Jordan's wrist to have a look as well.

"Does it look right to you?" Jordan asked her.

His mother shrugged. "I'm no lawyer."

Deputy Tam collected Jordan's cell phone, which caused smoke to blow out Jordan's ears and his face to turn red. Taking his cell was like detaching his arm.

"What am I supposed to do without my phone?" He watched Tam drop it into an evidence bag and hand it to a tech. "When will I get it back?"

"When we've finished with it," Guerrero said.

Jordan began wriggling his right heel up and down as he watched the deputies paw through his bedroom space that included a double-wide platform bed and four-high chest of drawers. A deputy examined Jordan's shirts and slacks, neatly hung on a piece of pipe. Another deputy dumped Jordan's dirty laundry out of a large cardboard box onto the garage concrete floor.

The front half of the garage served as Jordan's work space, and it was a disorganized muddle. Metal shelves climbed the walls and were stuffed with tools, reference books, manuals, and boxes of junk.

"You get things done in here?" Guerrero's eyes perused the mess.

"You ever see a picture of Einstein's study? He was a genius."

"My son, the genius." The woman folded her arms.

"I don't know what you think you're going to find. There's nothing here," Jordan complained.

"Where's your laptop?" Guerrero asked.

"Why?"

Deputy Tam immediately laid eyes on it. He lifted it off a cluttered work table. "Boss."

Guerrero nodded.

"Oh, come on," Jordan whined. "Stuff on there is personal."

Tam opened it. "We'll need the password."

Jordan shook his head. "You guys are so smart, you figure it out."

Tam moved aside and gestured for one of the tech boys to take a look. As the tech started working at the keyboard, Jordan's eyes shot daggers his way.

"Tell me something, Jordan." Guerrero strolled to the other side of the kid. "How did that video get leaked to the press?"

Jordan shrugged repeatedly, like an over-zealous marionette. "How should I know?"

"You set the cameras up. I'll bet you had a feed that went straight to your computer," Guerrero said.

Jordan pursed his lips, arms hugging his middle. He stared at the floor.

"We're going to examine everything. If that's what you did, we'll know," Guerrero told him.

Jordan raised his eyebrows. "It was Archibald's camera."

"It was evidence. Why leak it?"

"I thought it would be fun."

"Fun."

"Hey. You wouldn't even have video if it wasn't for me," Jordan asserted.

"That really isn't the point, now, is it?"

"Got it!" shouted the tech.

"Would you look at that? Guess we're pretty smart after all," Guerrero remarked.

Jordan guffawed. "It wasn't even hard."

"What was it? SmartAleck?" Guerrero asked.

Jordan's eyes narrowed and Guerrero laughed. "You're something else, kid."

The tech who was taking a preliminary look at Jordan's computer waved Guerrero over. They talked softly. Guerrero began to nod. "Where's the second remote, Jordan?" he called.

"There is no second remote."

Guerrero pointed at the monitor. "According to this there is. What'd you do with it?"

"I don't have a second remote."

"What'd you do with it?"

"I didn't do anything with it."

Guerrero looked at the screen. "Who's J?"

Jordan threw up his hands and then touched his chest. "Duhhh."

"You aren't referring to yourself here."

Jordan wouldn't look at him. "I want a lawyer."

"You haven't been arrested."

Jordan glowered. Guerrero spoke to the tech. "Bag it. I think we're done here."

The deputies stopped searching and filed out to their police cars. Guerrero lagged behind.

"I hope you didn't commit murder, Jordan. You're a smart kid, but murder's never smart."

"I didn't kill anybody."

"No? Hope not. But somebody did."

"People blame the ghost." Jordan puckered his lips in defiance.

"Yeah, I know. Is that what you were trying to do there with the camera angles askew?"

"Askew. That's a highfalutin word. Trying to prove you're a smart padre, Padre."

"Smart enough. We'll figure it out." Guerrero left the garage.

Jordan's mother patted her son on the shoulder and shuffled off to the house.

When Jordan was certain he was alone, he turned toward a stuffed, disorganized shelf that hadn't been searched and reached into a box shoved in the back. He withdrew a cheap cell phone.

"Yeah. You're smart enough to leave behind a burner, morons."

Jordan hadn't gotten around to disposing of it. He'd been naïve. It never occurred to him that the police would search his place, even though Jesse—Dr. J as he called him—had admonished over and over to get rid of the phone. He said: *No more counseling sessions. Get a new phone and a new number. And if you need to contact me, only do it with a burner. And get rid of the burner right after you call. We're cutting ties.*

Dr. J's nagging resulted in Jordan buying a new phone and getting a new number. He wanted the latest device anyway.

Jordan began dropping his dirty laundry back into the box as he remembered his first session with Dr. J. Now that he was in the thick of a police investigation, he wished he hadn't confessed to the therapist that he wondered what it would be like to kill someone. A regular psychologist would have asked him to share more and steer him away from that kind of thought. But Dr. J wasn't regular. He said they should explore the idea and then at some point—Jordan wasn't sure when—the doctor outright said it was important to act on his feelings as long as he found the right target.

The right target, as it turned out, was Archibald Bent, who had hired Jordan for his electronic and mechanical skills. A recent issue of *Popular Mechanics* included a story about genius Jordan, and that's how Archibald found him.

"Let's get creative," Dr. J said. "What could be your motive?"

Jordan wasn't even sure he wanted to kill anybody. He'd made the statement early on, mostly for shock value, and been led down the garden path. Sure, he'd killed a bothersome cat here and there. But it wasn't like he was bloodthirsty. The first cat had been an accident when he was only eight years old. He'd put it in a trash can and shut the lid. By the time Jordan remembered the cat was in the can, the animal had suffocated. The second casualty belonged to the neighbor. The cat kept pooping in his mother's roses, and she'd complained non-stop. His mother's voice could get very shrill. The third cat had been a stray that kept begging for food. Jordan killed it because he was bored and it was something to do.

Anyway, Jordan told himself, it was Dr. J who'd done the actual killing. He'd come up with the motive. Now that Jordan thought about it, the motive was what sent Dr. J into planning mode. He could hear him now:

Who is this guy, this Archibald? He writes about Double A? Does he ever write about her brother? No? But he writes about the singer because he hates her. Hates what she did to her brother's nightclub. Hmmmm. Murdering Archibald could really mess with people's heads. It would really mess with her brother's if we made it look like her ghost did it.

Jordan never understood the motive, but it was Dr. J who was calling the shots. Jordan actually felt bad that they'd killed Archie. He really did like the weirdo. He sighed. It was too late to feel bad about that now.

Jordan began to remake the bed. *If I go down for this, Dr. J's going down with me.* He tugged hard on a sheet. *If the police keep pushing me, I'm shoving back.*

He considered calling Dr. J to fill him in on the search warrant business. He squashed the idea, thinking Dr. J would rip him a new one and he didn't need that. But then again, he decided, Dr. J should probably know.

Chapter 12

Harmony nervously stood on the sidewalk outside the gates of Peter's mansion, fidgeting and doubting herself. Was she doing the right thing or was she crossing a line? Last night she'd had the most vivid dream in which Peter had killed himself. It scared her so badly that she decided to show up in person after having called once again and receiving no reply. With the anniversary of the nightclub tragedy, the trolls going after him on social media, and the memorial ceremony taking place at the disaster site, he could very well be contemplating death as a way out of his emotional pain. At least that's what she told herself.

The gate to the driveway was closed, the pedestrian access barred with a padlock. She couldn't casually saunter up to the door, but she hoped that since she was practically on his front step, using the intercom would help her get in.

She started to press the button, and immediately stopped. What if this dream was her subconscious creating a reason for her to reach out more aggressively because she wanted to see Peter and not because she really feared for his life? She felt conflicted. Jesse was right. She had crossed an emotional line. In all honesty, there'd been moments when she'd felt attracted to Peter and she'd denied it. So what was going on now? The dream had been vivid and she did fear for him. But was that all there was to it? She knew better than to act on any sort of personal affection she might feel.

Harmony's resolve to see Peter wavered and she took a step back. She looked at the massive mansion through the bars of the gate and found its size intimidating. The structure stood about a hundred feet away. She had a diagonal view with the right side the most visible. In some places, decades-old ivy wove up the walls from the ground to the second-floor roof. If it wasn't trimmed in the near future, windows would be covered. Trees were tall and the gardens overgrown. The iron fence surrounding the property and the out-of-control foliage acted together to create a fortress against the outside world. It gave the impression of a magnificent house sitting in a gigantic, but chaotic, nest.

Harmony had no idea if anyone was even home. She strained for a view into any of the windows, but the day's blue sky and white clouds reflecting in the glass made that difficult, until she thought she saw a face. From a window near the back where the ivy had yet to reach, she saw someone peering out. The features were obscure, and yet she got the impression it was a woman. Robina, perhaps? Who else would it be? Peter mentioned Robina all the time. He called her his girlfriend. Yes, she reminded herself, Peter had a girlfriend. A finger of guilt rode up her spine and she took a deep breath to chase the shame away. Coming here was not a good idea. In fact, it was a bad idea. It was time to go.

Harmony turned away from the house and immediately heard a clicking sound. She turned back. The gate was slowly opening. The woman she'd seen in the window must have decided to let her in. She hesitated, unsure of what to do. After a few more seconds of indecision, she walked past the gate and headed for the house. With every step, she wondered if she was making a mistake. When she reached the impressive double-door entryway she gawked. The doors were ten feet high and open.

"Okay. You've been invited in," she whispered.

Her heart began to race.

"Hello," she said as she stepped inside.

No one came to greet her. She cleared her throat and called, "Peter!" After giving him time to answer, she called out again. "It's Dr. McKenna." There was still no response.

She saw no one anywhere. Outside there'd been no sign of any hired help. Inside there were no cooks, no housekeepers, no friends. Most importantly, there was no Peter. But someone had to have opened the gate and the front door.

"Hello! Is anybody home?"

For a second she thought she heard a faint "hello" back, after which, the house remained completely still.

"Hello," she called again. This time she heard nothing.

A round glass table, eight feet across, sat dead center in the foyer. It was the sort of thing one would see in a fancy hotel lobby. It supported a tall, oval vase that begged to be filled with an impressive arrangement of flowers. Sadly, it sat gaping and hungry. Harmony felt a sense of neglect. The white marble floor needed to be polished. Nothing shone.

Harmony stepped around the table, then jumped at the sound of the front doors shutting with a bang. The noise boomed and reverberated, taking a couple of seconds before quieting into an unsettling silence. She swallowed, her senses on edge. The lighting was adequate, but not strong, and she suddenly felt as if she had entered a very large, empty tomb—Peter's tomb, where he had been doing his best to survive.

Stop with the imaginative bullshit. Just stop!

"Peter, the door was open," she called, not just to alert him, but to fill the space with sound and life. "Did you open the gate for me? Where are you? Would you please come out so we can talk?"

If he was home, he didn't acknowledge her. What about Robina? Was she there? Had she opened the gate and the doors? Was she the face in the upstairs window? The more Harmony thought about it, the more she thought that might be the case. But then, why didn't she answer?

Harmony stared at the sweeping set of stairs that created an elegant path to the second floor. They seemed to invite her up. She sucked the inside of her mouth as if the soft tissue were a baby's pacifier and wondered if she should she be so bold as to climb them. She'd come this far . . .

"I'm coming up," she called out, giving whoever was home time to tell her to stop. No one did.

She began to climb, her hand clutching the banister as if it were a life preserver. What was she so afraid of? It was just a house. Peter's house. What was she expecting? To be ambushed by home invaders? Or maybe come face to face with his sister's ghost, the one he'd said was too horrifying to describe. She didn't believe in ghosts.

"Robina? Are you here? I'd like to meet you."

Silence.

She took the steps with care, finally reaching the landing, and wondered which way to go. A hallway led to the right and the left. The light was dim and shadows were softly gray. Everything felt lonely. Peter's sad energy and aching heart had permeated his home.

She remained still, unable to decide which way to go.

Just move. Check every door.

This was crazy. What was she doing? She wasn't sure, but for some reason she needed to continue. She took a step to the right when the creak of a floor board behind her caused her to twist in the opposite direction.

"Hello?" she said.

The hallway for this route was longer. It stretched before her and made an L-shaped turn. Perhaps the creak was a hint to come this way instead. Did she believe that? Not really. But then she could hardly believe she was an intruder in Peter's house.

She came to a door, opened it, and found a guest bedroom. Exploring it, she found it had its own bathroom and dressing area. Twice more she happened upon doors that led to empty guest suites. Another door led to what could only be described as a reading room or library, filled with books and comfortable seating areas.

At the end of the hall, buried in darker shadows, was one last door. It looked menacing, and yet it beckoned her. She swallowed as she stared.

Probably just another guest room. No need to bother with it.

She frowned. Was this the room with the window where she'd seen that face?

Her heart began to pound. Someone—or something—was behind that door.

Something? You're letting your imagination run away with you.

She stood for a while, taking deep breaths, wondering why she continued to stay in the house when fear filled her every pore. She had no answer. All she knew was she also felt compelled.

There's probably a back staircase, she told herself. *You'll be fine. You can make a quick getaway if you need to.*

Getaway? Get away from what, exactly?

She took a gulp of air. There was no turning back. She needed to know what was behind that door. Curiosity could be a greater motivator then fear.

She took a step and then another.

Eight feet away . . . six feet . . . now four. Two more steps and she was less than an arm's length from the knob. She could take hold if she wanted. Her arm remained at her side and her heart beat so quickly it could out-pace an alarm bell.

What do you want to go in there for?

I don't know. I don't know.

You'll be trespassing.

She almost laughed. *Invalid point. I've been trespassing for a while. If the door is locked, I'll leave.*

But none of the other the rooms had been locked. What made her think this one would be any different? She continued to hesitate as she analyzed what the hell she was doing.

This is the point of no return. If you go inside, you'll know something you didn't know before. It will alter your view of the world forever.

What? You don't know that.

Her hand went to her chest and she held it there.

There are more things in heaven and earth, Harmony, than are dreamt of in your philosophy.

She believed that. Of course, she believed that. But was she ready for some life-changing experience? Maybe she liked being the way she was—believing what she believed.

The doorknob made a metallic sound when it turned. She hadn't turned it. She was still undecided and scared. The door squeaked open a mere inch. All she had to do was give it a push.

Maybe I already passed the point of no return when I stepped inside the house.

Cold energy pour through the one-inch gap. The air felt charged with electricity. Strands of hair rose straight up from her head the way it once had when she visited the Grand Canyon. She detected the faintest scent of gasoline coming from the room.

She looked at her arm. It was gooseflesh. This wasn't imaginative fear mongering. She was experiencing something tangible. It was a summons. She had to go in.

Harmony reached out and gave the door a nudge. It swung wide, as if she'd shoved it. Now the scent of gasoline was stronger, and she could hear the shower running in the bathroom. Her heart fell. She was intruding on a person, not a mystifying thing. She was about to infringe on someone's privacy.

She shook her head. She didn't have to infringe on anybody. She could turn around and run. Only she didn't want to. She wanted to know who was in the shower. She had to know.

Slowly, she stepped toward the dressing area with its closed bathroom door. She felt like Nancy Drew about to solve a mystery. Only she wasn't a beloved character in a book that would remain a teen forever and exist safely within the pages of a series. She was made of flesh and blood and was about to come face to face . . . with what?

The supernatural.

That thought stopped her dead where she stood.

Supernatural? Who said anything about the supernatural?

You just did. And your hair is still standing on end. Remember the point of no return? Remember you'll be changed forever?

She felt like she'd already changed. She opened the bathroom door. The water streamed full force and it had steamed the room like a sauna. The shower door was clear glass, but even though it had fogged up, she saw no shadow. No one was inside the stall.

She heard a squeaking sound and looked at the long mirror that stretched above the vanity. An unseen finger was writing in the haze:

G . . . o . . . s . . . e . . . e . . D . . . a . . . r . . . i . . . u . . . s

She stared. What? *Go see . . .* She didn't know any Darius.

The water shut off. The fog on the mirror lessened with each passing second, and she found herself unable to move. Her heart no longer pounded like a hammer on an anvil, but still it exerted itself more than it should. She stared at the evaporating mist, letters slowly dissolving. Suddenly, the smell of gasoline intensified, creating an awful stench, and a woman stood beside her, both of them reflected in the silver nitrate glass. *Andrea.* Everyone knew the beautiful Double A. Only her face did not remain beautiful. It morphed into the face of a woman who had burned in a fire—blackened, ghastly, terrifying, surreal.

We're both scarred, Harmony heard in her head.

She whipped around to find no one there.

Had she just seen what she thought she'd seen? A spirit? A spectre? A phantom? A . . . Yes, she had. Double A was a ghost, just as Peter had said.

Oh my God!

The stench of gasoline vanished. Double A was gone.

"And I'm gone, too," she eagerly announced.

She'd had enough. She ran out of the suite, down the hall, her heart pounding so hard she thought it might burst. She tripped and fell. Glancing over her shoulder, she saw no one, but that didn't lesser her fear. She jumped to her feet and continued to the stairs. Clutching the banister, afraid she'd trip again, she made her way to the bottom of the stairs.

That door better not be locked!
It wasn't.
She ran out of the house.

A thousand questions raced through Harmony's mind as she jogged for the gate, only to see that it was closed. How was she supposed to get out? She paused, turned, and looked at the house.

Had she really experienced what she thought she'd experienced? *Oh yes.* She wasn't going to second-guess this. She wasn't going to shove it into her subconscious and try to convince herself that she'd imagined it. The spirit of Double A had appeared to her.

And she had given her a message. Was Andrea actually trying to help her brother, not destroy him as Peter thought? Obviously people gave themselves explanations when they didn't have all the facts.

Well, do you have all the facts? she asked herself.

With a deep sigh, she gave her full attention to the gate. There was no squeezing through. There wasn't enough space. She looked around and saw a curved stone bench in what might have been a charming garden area of Peter's grounds if it weren't overgrown with a tangle of wisteria, birds of paradise, creeping ivy, and wild roses.

Nature gone amok.

Harmony walked over and sat. Her heartbeat returned to normal. Now that she was outside and a safe distance from the house, she felt okay. But Peter needed to have a word with his gardener, or hire one. The aged palm trees were too high in the sky to provide any shade. The purple jacaranda did a nice job. It also did a decent job of dropping blooms on Harmony's head, something the beautiful, but messy, trees did best.

Now what? It never occurred to her when she'd come through the gate that she'd be stuck in need of rescue. She took out her cell phone and thought about leaving a message for Peter. She could explain her plight. It was doubtful, however, that it would do any good. He never got back to her.

There was Jesse. But he'd gone out of town and she didn't want to confess she'd gone to Peter's house. He didn't understand their relationship. Or maybe he understood better than she did and that was the problem.

Who else did she know who could bring some cutters and lop off the lock to the gate? The only names that came to mind were people she'd lost touch with, and that was a sobering thought. Was Jesse the only person she had to call in a crisis?

Peter would have to come home some time and she could corner him. She could tell him she saw Andrea, which would mean confessing that she'd gone inside his house. Was she really prepared to do that?

She grimaced and put the phone down just as the gate began to slide. She stood up and watched Peter's white BMW roll onto the drive. The convertible top was down. Peter was glancing toward the passenger side as if he saw someone. He looked like he was talking to the invisible man.

Another ghost? Funny how quickly one could change one's point of view.

She almost chased after him, but stopped. It would mean confessing she'd been in his house uninvited. Well, she'd been invited by Andrea, it seemed. Was that a good excuse? Showing up at his house meant she'd stalked him and that might make matters worse. He might take offense. She needed to pick the time and place to share with him what had happened.

She caught sight of the gate, saw that it was halfway closed. She made a run for it, squeezing through the shrinking opening, escaping to the outside world in the nick of time.

Chapter 13

The forensics team was certainly invested in the Archibald Bent case. They were making the evidence analysis a priority. Guerrero didn't even have to press. Standing in the lab, surrounded by three excited techs, he had to remind them to talk one at a time as they eagerly shared with him what they'd found on Jordan's laptop and phone.

"The guy's a moron. A smart moron, but a moron just the same," Melvin said. "Aside from that one lame password, he didn't try to hide a thing."

"Look here." Anton pointed at a schematic on the laptop. "Look what he wrote at the top. Archie's Party. Remote number 2. Remote number 2!"

"I see that," Guerrero replied quietly, amused at their enthusiasm. "You solved the case."

"Okay, no," conceded Teresa. "But it's all there. How the remotes worked. The script for how the murder would go down. In black and white. I mean honestly. What murderer does that?"

"Yeah," said Guerrero. "But he has an alibi so he has an accomplice. The phone didn't give anyone up?"

"There are lots of contacts with the letter J. James. Jerrod. Jacob. Julie. Jennifer. And that's just the first names."

Guerrero rubbed his temples. "I'll get Thacker and Haynes to check out the Js. No one came across a burner in that garage?"

"No one gave us one."

"Maybe I called it too soon. I'll send someone back over to have a second look. Jordan seems pretty inexperienced. He probably thinks one pass and we're done."

"There is one weird thing," Melvin offered. "And maybe he just left it out of the script."

"What's that?"

"It calls for Double A's laugh and we found a recording on the laptop he'd taken from YouTube of her laughing. But the script doesn't call for her to say anything and she says 'There's nothing I could do.' We had the voice analyzed. It's her. It's Double A."

"Well, okay." Guerrero frowned. "He added it somewhere along the line. Let's not go down Jordan's rabbit hole and start thinking there's a ghost." Guerrero took out a ginger chew. "All right. Well. Good job here. My thing now is to find a motive. I mean, why kill this guy?"

All the techs concurred.

"Yeah. There's no motive on the laptop."

"None at all."

"Wish we'd found one."

"Not that there has to be one these days, but it would be nice," Guerrero said. He ambled out of the lab, thinking about his next move. He could put Jordan in the hot seat and he was sure he'd get something more. He'd do that eventually. But for now, his next move was that nightclub memorial. He'd nose around and see who was there. He also wanted to talk to Pete, the guy so many people hated. As far as he could tell, there was no connection between Pete, Archibald, and Jordan—but you never knew. Every angle needed to be explored.

Guerrero went home to change his clothes.

***

Of course they were trespassing, and Wayne knew he could call the police and have the memorial shut down. The organizers might have gotten a permit to assemble, but they couldn't get one to be on private property and with so many people present they had certainly done that. Also, there had to be close to a thousand people present which was surely over the limit.

He supposed he didn't mind as long as everyone behaved and was respectful. These were the loved ones of those who had lost their lives in the fire, and if they needed to still express their grief after five years, who was he to say they should be over it? Pete certainly wasn't over it. If he, Wayne, had lost a son or daughter, he wouldn't be over it. The only thing that angered him was the way they took their heartache out on his business partner and friend. Pete had not started the fire. Andrea had done that all on her own. There was even video to prove it. But people loved their conspiracy theories. Elvis hasn't left the building. We faked the moon landing. The holocaust never happened. Pete started the fire for the insurance money and killed his sister.

Horse pucky. Hog manure. Bullshit!

It might not go down as an epic moment in history, but it was still a lie.

People held their phones high above their heads, the flashlight apps causing them to beam like mini spotlights aimed toward the sky. Right now everyone was singing *My Immortal* by Evanescence.

"Your presence still lingers here . . . ," they sang in unison.

It was a moving sight, even with the depressing view of the burnt-out nightclub partially erect in the background. Someone had rigged blue spotlights on the building so it could be seen in the darkness. Yes, it was still there after five years because Wayne had been forced to play tiddlywinks with the insurance company. They'd reckoned they could outmaneuver him into accepting less than what they owed, but Wayne was no fool. He had the law and excellent recordkeeping on his side. He and Pete hadn't paid a fortune in insurance over the years to have them cheat.

Wayne moved out of the path of a television news crew. There were also independent bloggers and social media journalists roaming about. The last thing Wayne needed was to be recognized and interviewed. He'd decided to come see the event for himself, and also, it was a way of paying his respects. That was the extent of it. He had no desire for publicity.

"Mr. Hoffman? Wayne Hoffman?"

Oh hell, thought Wayne. He'd been spotted. He turned around to find a woman in her early thirties standing in front of him. She was lovely, even with the obvious scar etched into the side of her face.

"Hello," said Wayne. "Yes, I'm Mr. Hoffman, but I'd prefer not to be interviewed—"

"I'm not a reporter."

"You're not."

"No. I'm Peter's therapist. Harmony McKenna." She offered her hand and he took it.

"Oh!" Wayne almost smiled.

"Well, *was* his therapist."

Wayne sighed. "He's playing that game again."

"No. I think something happened. I don't know what. He ghosted me." She chuckled. She hadn't meant to make a pun.

Wayne smiled this time. "He told you about the ghost. That's good. He didn't tell any of the others."

"I wondered if you could tell me how he's doing."

"I saw him a couple days ago. He looked better. I guess I have you to thank for that."

"I don't even know what I'm doing here," Harmony said. "I know there's no way Peter would have ever come. I wasn't even looking for you."

"No?"

"But since I did run into you, I was hoping you could encourage Peter to contact me when you see him. He's free to stop having me be his therapist, I'd just like us to part ways with, I don't know, some closure."

"Of course. He needs to see someone. Otherwise he's like a ship without a rudder. He just flounders."

"Yeah." She bit her bottom lip. "It occurred to me, I mean I was wondering. Has Peter ever mentioned someone named Darius?"

"Darius? As in Rucker? No. Never. Why? Is this person important to his therapy?"

"To tell you the truth, I have no idea. It's just a name that came up and I thought I'd ask since I saw you here. But apparently you don't know him either. Okay, then. It was nice to meet you."

"Do you have a card?" Wayne asked. "In case I have a reason to contact you."

"Sure." Harmony withdrew one from a silver case and handed it to him. "And perhaps I could have yours, you know. Just in case."

***

Detective Guerrero couldn't say he'd gathered any intel as he wandered among the crowd. Dressed in his favorite chartreuse Hawaiian shirt, he supposed he still looked like a cop—one on vacation, but still a policeman. He made small talk here and there between sets of songs and between the speeches some people gave, those who chose to mount the platform and share their feelings of grief and nostalgia. Melancholia hung in the air. This was definitely not a celebration of anyone's life. This was a pity party, one that included sentiments of blame. He had no doubt if Peter Ashton were to have shown up, they'd have tarred and feathered him and run him out of town on a rail. That was an old-fashioned way of saying someone would have hurt him.

The detective was getting more and more eager to meet this Pete and hear his side of the story. He would also like to know what the man thought about the murder of Archibald Bent. What did he have to say about his sister being a ghost?

He didn't see Pete, which he thought was a good thing, but he did spot Wayne Hoffman, the business partner. Right now Wayne was speaking to a young woman with a scar on her face. The detective wondered how that had happened. They were in the process of bidding each other good-bye. After she walked away, Guerrero took the opportunity to approach the man.

"Hello. Mr. Hoffman?"

"Yes," Wayne responded, his tone inferring he was unhappy about the intrusion.

Guerrero was used to people expressing their displeasure at seeing him, although it was always because they knew he was a cop. He presumed Mr. Hoffman didn't know—yet.

"I wondered if I might ask you some informal questions. I'm a detective working the Archibald Bent murder case. You may have heard of it. My name's Guerrero."

"Everyone's heard of it. A very bizarre way to murder somebody. Why would you release a video like that?"

"We didn't."

"Ah. I see. Then again, I don't see. Why question me?"

"The Double A angle."

"Because her brother is my business partner and the murder victim went on a rant about her on social media. That's a rather tenuous connection, wouldn't you say?"

"We have to look at everything. So you're confirming that Pete, your business partner, is Double A's brother."

Wayne's face turned to stone. "Why does that matter?"

"I don't know that it does. I'd like to talk to him, though. Do you think he's seen the video?"

"I honestly don't know. He does his best to avoid any controversies in the media when it comes to her."

Guerrero glanced about. "Yeah. People seem to have a lot of negative, unsubstantiated opinions."

"You noticed. It's unfortunate and completely unfair." Wayne took a breath and glanced about. "Well. If that's all."

"Just one more thing." Guerrero took out his business card. Hesitated, and took out two. "Could you encourage Pete to call me? I need to talk to him. I promise I'll be as delicate and respectful as possible."

"I can ask." Wayne took the cards, gave the detective a nod, and walked away.

Guerrero watched him go. Maybe it was time to lean on Jordan. This time of night a visit would surprise him. Catch him off guard. Open him up. It was known to work sometimes. Jordan wouldn't be a hard nut to crack.

When the detective arrived at Jordan's, the garage door was closed and there didn't appear to be any light coming from the gap at the ground. He checked his watch. It wasn't all that late. Ten. He could see a television glow through curtains in the living room of the house. He knocked on the front door and called out. "Mrs. Lyman? It's Detective Guerrero."

It took a minute, but the door opened and Jordan's mother looked at him with vodka-soaked eyes, glass in hand. "What are you doing here?" she asked, leaning against the door for support.

"I need to talk to your son again."

"Now?" She knitted her brow.

"That's why I'm here."

"Well, he isn't." She slopped her drink when she nodded with a little too much animation. "Here. He isn't here."

"Where is he?"

"With . . . I don't know. Do you want to come in?" She took an unsteady step back.

"No. I think I should . . . I'll stay out here."

"Suit yourself." She steadied herself, using the door. "You know, that son of mine, he lies all the time."

"Does he?"

"Yeah. Well, to me. He lies to me." She poked her chest with her free hand.

"What did he lie to you about?"

"He said . . . Actually he snuck in the house. Sometimes I fall asleep in front of the TV. But I woke up and caught him just as he was leaving without saying anything." She took a sip from her glass.

"And he lied to you, how?"

"He said he was going to see his shrink. Ha! He stopped seeing that man a long time ago. Months!" The vodka slopped again when she jerked her arm upward. She frowned. "You're making me waste my . . . drink. Very expensive stuff, my drink. Inflation, you know."

"Where is this shrink? What's his name?"

She shook her head. "I don't remember. Somewhere over the rainbow."

"You never met him."

"Nah. Jordan's a big boy. He went on his own. Doctor J! That's what Jordan called him. Yeah. Yeah. Doctor J." She closed the door before Guerrero could ask any more questions. And before she fell over.

***

Jordan's car was not the best. It was sixteen years old with two hundred and sixty thousand miles on it. The silver paint had blistered off long ago. But it ran. Jordan was enough of a mechanic he could keep the old Corolla trucking on down the road and pass smog to boot. If only he knew how to turn his genius into steady cash, he'd have the best of both worlds: work that was play and money to live high on the hog.

He'd made it as far as Interstate 15 and was headed up the Cajon Pass. He only drove this way when he felt the itch to gamble in Vegas, and that didn't happen too often because of that cash flow issue he had.

Trucks were thick in the right-hand lane, sometimes in the right two lanes. The speeders kept to the left. Or they were supposed to. It didn't always happen that way. There were always a few vehicles that weaved in and out or got on Jordan's tail because Jordan didn't speed. He stayed in the middle lane and maintained the speed limit, which angered the speedsters who thought it was his job to get out of their way. They would get very close, then whip around within an inch of Jordan's bumper. At least the pass was open and moving tonight. No accidents. No fires. Jordan yawned. Oncoming headlights made him sleepy, and unfortunately it was another hour to Dr. J's spread in Lucerne Valley. Why the doc insisted Jordan come tonight was a mystery, but he'd gotten up in his face about it. Jordan had made the mistake of using the burner phone one last time to call and say the police had shown up a second time to take a look around, but he'd remembered to really hide the phone this time.

"Hide! You were supposed to dispose of it." Jordan blanked on the rest of Dr. J's rant. The cursing session ticked Jordan off so badly, he decided not to dispose of the phone. Nope. He kept it. The police were hot on Jordan's tail and like he'd already decided, if he was going down, Dr. J was going down as well. Fair was fair.

When the therapist became civil again, he told Jordan he had a job for him and he needed him to come to his place in Lucerne Valley tonight. Jordan was skeptical. It could be that he just wanted to yell at him in person. But cash was king, as Jordan always said, and he needed to take a chance. He'd never been to Lucerne Valley and wrote down the directions. The police had taken his cell. He couldn't do things the normal way and put the address in a phone. Well, unless he stole into the house and took his mom's. Yeah. That's what he needed to do. He wasn't driving to Lucerne Valley without a smart phone.

So that's what he did. Sneaked in the house and snatched the old drunk's cell.

***

The moment Jordan told him he still had the burner, Jesse knew the kid was a loose end and had to go. Pleasure killings were more satisfying than ones committed out of necessity, but Jesse had to do what Jesse had to do. How could people be so brilliant and stupid at the same time? Jesse had never figured that out, but in his experience it was a common phenomenon. Jordan fell into that category.

He knew exactly what he was going to do. He'd toss an envelope of cash on the dining room table and tell Jordan it was his after the job was done, maybe entice him by saying, half now, half when it was complete. Surely Jordan would happily follow him to the mine, where Jesse would slit his lily white throat.

A mixture of peace from knowing what he was going to do and excitement from knowing he was going to get to do it soothed Jesse. Wasn't life grand? He even felt like talking to Harmony. She'd done the usual, left a few text messages throughout the day which he didn't answer. He liked the idea that he was torturing her with his lack of response. Then the thought hit him like a boxer's left hook. What if he wasn't torturing her? What if she didn't care?

The insecure, vengeful Jesse reared its ugly head. He grabbed his phone and went into the bedroom where he stretched out on the bed, one ankle crossed over the other. He took a deep breath and called.

"Jesse," Harmony answered.

"Did I wake you?" He spoke softly.

"No. I have the TV on, just lazing."

"What'd you do today? Did Pete ever call you back?"

"No. He's still missing in action."

"And how do you feel about that?"

"Ha. Ha. Don't start with the doctor lingo. You know how I feel about it."

"Still?"

"Well, I'd rather know what happened than remain in the dark. I went to that memorial for the victims of the nightclub disaster."

Anger shot from Jesse's chest to his throat. For a second he couldn't talk. "Why? Hoping he'd be there?"

"I knew he *wouldn't* be there. I don't know. It's a process, letting go of his story."

She was still consumed with Pete, he could tell, and that would never be acceptable to Jesse. "But you're letting go?"

She hesitated.

"What aren't you telling me?"

"Nothing. There's nothing to tell. Why are you so hung up on this?"

Jesse didn't answer. Instead his attention was drawn to the sound of the doorbell. Jordan had arrived for his final curtain. "I have to go." He hung up abruptly.

When Jesse opened the front door, he found Jordan leaning against one of the porch posts, wearing a stupid grin. "Ahh. What's up doc?"

"All you need is a carrot," Jesse responded. "Get in here."

Jordan entered, a dopey expression on his face. "So. What's up? For real?"

Jesse raised his hand. "Wait for me in the dining room. Right through there." He pointed before he rushed into the bedroom and grabbed a stack of cash from a drawer.

That ought'a do it.

He didn't have an envelope handy, but thought the sight of actual legal tender would be more effective anyway. He picked up the knife he'd placed on the dresser after deciding he needed to kill Jordan and slipped it in an inside pocket of his jacket, which he shrugged into.

Jesse entered the dining room to find Jordan moseying aimlessly, hands shoved in his pockets. Jesse slapped the money on the dining room table. "Five hundred dollars."

Jordan looked less than impressed. "It probably cost that much just to drive up here with the price of gas in California these days."

"No need to be cute. I'll make this job worth your while."

"I don't have to kill anybody this time, do I?"

"That was a one-time, uh, experiment."

"It was an experiment, wasn't it? We did it because you said I should explore my feelings."

"Did I say that? I don't remember saying that."

"Oh, come on, man. That's exactly what you said. And we haven't even talked about it. All you *did* say was 'we have to cut ties.' So what am I doing here, anyway? Not cutting ties?"

Jordan pulled out one of the chairs and plopped his butt down, his mouth drawn into a pout.

Jesse decided it was time for some finesse. The money wasn't doing its job. "Okay. Since you're here—" His heart nearly stopped. He'd been reckless asking Jordan to drive to his house in the heat of anger without making sure of a few things. "You did say the cops took your phone."

"They sure did."

"So you don't have it."

"Nope."

"And you didn't tell your mother where you were going tonight?"

"No." Jordan bit at a hangnail.

Jesse took the chair next to Jordan's. He leaned in with his forearms on his knees. "All right. Then let's do this. How did killing Archibald Bent make you feel?"

"Let's get one thing straight. I didn't actually kill him, you did. You dressed up as the executioner. You worked the remote to get him all freaked out. You locked his head in the guillotine and you pulled the cord that released the blade. You! You cut off his head."

"But it was your mechanical skills that allowed all that to happen. So, again, I'll ask. How did killing Archibald Bent make you feel?"

Jordan jumped to his feet. "Shitty! Why didn't we kill someone I didn't like?"

"Do you have someone in mind?" Jesse felt the corners of his mouth turn upward. He was completely amused.

"How about *you*?" The expression on Jordan's face made Jesse laugh.

"All right. I get it. The cops are breathing down your neck and you're mad at me. What you don't understand is you just have to remain cool. You have an alibi. You weren't there. So what can they do to you?"

"I don't know," Jordan mumbled. "Nothing, I guess."

"So cheer up. Let me tell you about this job I have for you. Huh? Make some easy cash and you'll be good to go."

Jordan looked at the money on the table. "I can tell you right now five hundred dollars won't cut it."

"I said I'd make it worth your while. Five hundred down. Five hundred when you complete the job. How does that sound?"

"What's the job?"

"I need you to make something for me."

"What?"

"A door."

"You can buy a door."

"I need this door to open and close remotely. And it needs to camouflage an opening."

"What kind of opening?"

"Well, that's what I need to show you. So come on. Let's go. Follow me." Jesse headed out. Jordan stayed put. "Well, come on."

"Outside?"

"Yes."

"In the dark."

"The sun is facing the other side of the planet."

"No."

"Jordan. I have a lantern that'll light the way." If he had to manhandle Jordan he would. The kid was scrawny and wouldn't stand a chance. But Jesse didn't want to do that. He wanted everything nice and organized. If he could kill him in the mine, that would be a plus. However, just getting him close would suffice. "Six hundred down," Jesse said.

"You must really want that door."

"I do. Name your price. But you need to come now."

"Why can't I look in the morning?"

Frustration was quickly consuming Jesse. He needed to change tactics. "Okay. You don't want the job, forget it—"

"I didn't say that."

Jesse put his hands on his hips and looked at Jordan. "Then you're coming."

The kid didn't look happy. "Two thousand dollars!" he blurted.

"And that includes your gas."

Jordan burst out laughing. "Sure. Where're we going?"

"Like I said. Follow me."

Jesse walked to the large bonus room and out the slider. He took hold of the large lantern he'd placed outside and turned it on. Immediately small moths and insects began to swirl. He started walking and could tell from the footsteps he heard, Jordan wasn't far behind. He felt for the knife in his pocket and excitement raised his pulse. Another kill. That would make three in one month. Four if you counted the dog. He smiled and began to walk faster.

"Hey!" Jordan shouted. "What's the rush?"

Jesse slowed his pace. "Sorry. But keep up, will ya?"

"Nah."

Jesse heard Jordan stop. Jesse turned around. They were still very close to the house. What was Jordan's problem now?

"I'm tired," Jordan said.

It only took Jesse's long legs six quick strides to reach Jordan.

"Well, don't look so pissed. I—"

Jesse's plunge of the knife between Jordan's ribs pierced both lungs, allowing blood to rush in. Jordan staggered backward, unable to scream. His eyes were pools of bewilderment and fear. Jesse watched and waited. Jordan coughed and blood spilled from his mouth and nose, an ugly sight that titillated Jesse. He stared in fascination as Jordan tottered to and fro. The kid even reached out with an arm as if asking Jesse to help him. It seemed like forever, but it only took a minute for Jordan to drop to his back and stop moving. His eyes stared skyward, but he saw no stars. He saw nothing at all.

***

Harmony jolted straight off the bed. There was Darius, in living color on her bedroom TV. He'd been at the memorial. He'd been interviewed by the local news. Below his face, across the bottom of the screen, a caption read: Darius—Spiritual Healer.

Harmony forgot all about her strange exchange with Jesse and turned up the volume.

"There are a lot of mourners here today," the twenty-something female reporter said.

The cameraman began panning. Hundreds of people could be seen crowding the sidewalk, even blocking the street. The remains of the burnt-down nightclub rose in the background about thirty yards away. The camera focused on it and zoomed. A metal fence protected the structure from the curious and protected the curious from possibly being hurt if they tried to explore. Handmade signs with words of remembrance and love were attached to the fence with zip ties and hooks. Debris from the fire had long since been cleared away, but the foundation remained, as did some of the less-damaged walls. The smoke had left its mark. Black stains rose from pane-less window openings.

"And your name is?" the reporter asked Darius.

"Darius."

"And you came to pay your respects to those who lost their lives."

"I did. I did." He spoke softly and made a little bow with prayerful hands.

Harmony frowned. Who was this guy? Why in the world would Andrea's ghost want her to meet him? He came off as strange—pretentious with weird mannerisms. But then, believing a ghost had given her a message was a little strange.

"And there is much discord. I wanted to come as a peaceful presence because positive energy is so important."

The reporter eyed the surroundings. "The attendees seem very peaceful."

"They are not at peace. And many of them direct insensitive barbs to my client because of their misbeliefs."

"Client!" Harmony's frown grew deeper. Was he talking about Peter? Did this man consider Peter his client? Peter was talking to him, but not her? Mixed emotions ran the gamut, head to toe.

Am I jealous?

You bet I am.

"Who is your client?" the reporter asked.

"Oh, that I cannot say." Darius looked directly into the camera. "I can say this. Andrea wants someone to find me. That is another reason for me to be here. And, Andrea is sorry. She would like to make amends." He smiled and bowed. "*Namaste.*" Darius walked out of camera range.

"Okay," said the reporter. "I don't know what that was all about. Let's see if we can find—"

Harmony hit the off button. She was stunned. Had Andrea really arranged all this? It was crazy. Unbelievable! And yet, she couldn't see any other explanation. Hells bells. She was buying into it!

Harmony hopped onto her computer and went searching. She found Darius on Yelp. He had no reviews. The blurb read:

Healing with Darius.

Expert clairvoyant and spiritual healer with decades of experience. Namaste.

There was a button for potential clients to provide contact information and ask for an appointment.

"No way." Harmony frowned. Even with her paranormal experience in Peter's house, even after seeing Darius on TV, she couldn't wrap her head around this guy being anything other than a fake.

She sat and stared at the screen. Well. What was she going to do? Believe that a ghost had set this up and contact Darius, or forget the whole thing?

She couldn't forget the whole thing. This guy knew Peter. This guy considered Peter a client.

She began to pace the room. People did this sort of supernatural stuff every day. But she wasn't one of them. Why should she start dabbling now?

You know why, she told herself.

I'm being manipulated.

You saw a ghost.

Did I? Did I really?

Oh, what did she have to lose? She clicked on the contact button and provided her email address and phone number. She wrote in the message box:

I'm Harmony. Andrea gave me a message to "Go see Darius." That's you, right? I don't believe in this woo-woo crap. I really don't. But here I am contacting you. I assume this about Peter.

She left it at that, shut off the computer and her phone. She would check for messages in the morning. Right now everything was too confusing and annoying. Sleep was her friend. In this moment, she couldn't deal with anything more. She had told herself she wasn't going to second-guess her experience at Peter's, that she wasn't going to shove it into her subconscious and try to convince herself she'd imagined it. But that was exactly what she wanted to do.

She climbed into bed and prayed sleep would come soon.

***

Jesse spent most of the night cleaning up his mess. He used a wheelbarrow to transport Jordan to the mine. Then he dragged him to the pit. He checked Jordan's pockets before tossing him over the side and was happy to see that Jordan hadn't lied. He was absent a cell phone.

Next, Jesse needed to dispose of Jordan's car. Hawkeye hadn't been a problem. Hawkeye didn't have a car. He'd always used

Jesse's truck. The caretaker had been a loner, and didn't own much. Jesse had quickly disposed of Hawkeye's effects, including a photo he'd found of the man's daughter. Hawkeye had identified her on the back of the picture. Jesse didn't recall Hawkeye ever talking about a daughter. But if Jesse were being honest, he never listened to what the hired hand rambled on about. Jesse decided to toss the picture along with everything else. When the police came around, and they would eventually, they didn't need the photo as a lead.

Jordan's Corolla was a problem. Anywhere he dumped it, he needed a way to get back afterward. The aqueduct in Hesperia was a favorite among thieves who stripped cars and dumped what was left. But Jesse wasn't familiar enough with where he should go to do that and nixed the idea. He ultimately decided to hitch the car to his truck, tow the thing to some desolate spot where it wasn't likely to be found, and leave it. The Chevy Colorado was perfect for off-road terrain. He'd merely drive for however long felt right and abandon the piece of junk. Happy with his solution, Jesse hitched the Corolla to the pickup and took off.

He stuck to dirt roads for a long while, listening to the crunch of the gravel beneath the tires as he sped faster than he should have with the car attached. The truck was plenty sturdy, and the handling was great, but with the Corolla anchored to the rear, he felt more jostling than he anticipated. High beams brightened the way while moths fluttered across his path.

At first he'd dreaded the task of disposing of the car, but now he felt exhilarated. This was another thing he would get away with. Jesse gave no thought to poor Jordan lying amid the rubble, bones, and bodies in the mine pit. As far as he was concerned, his partnership with Jordan was a beautiful thing of the past with the added perk of an ideal ending.

He finally came to an area of the desert that spoke to him, steered to the right, and left the gravel road. Now he had to maneuver the creosote bushes and Joshua trees that thrived on the desert landscape. Jesse let loose with a heady scream knowing no one but the coyotes could hear. The black sky, full moon, and extreme haste made him feel alive and he couldn't contain himself. What could be better than committing murder and making a clean getaway?

His recklessness nearly cost him when he came up too fast on a three-foot-high boulder and had to make a sharp twist to the right. The truck missed the obstruction, but the Corolla did not. The sound of metal crunching and buckling caused his heart to nearly burst. He laughed out loud and slowed the truck to a stop. What a ride!

Overcome with a mixture of euphoria, adrenaline, and an intense desire for more, he let loose with a piercing scream.

Gulping for air, he calmed himself and reviewed the situation. This was as good a place as any to abandon Jordan's car. He turned off the ignition and relieved the truck of its load. He climbed back into the Chevy, swung around and headed for home, his trusty GPS guiding him all the way.

Chapter 14

Alone in the break room, Detective Guerrero stared into the abyss that was his cup of black coffee and tapped on the side of his World's Best Granddad mug. They'd come up empty with Jordan's phone. It had been recently purchased and didn't include people he'd called prior to two months ago. They would see what the carrier's records said about his cell number or any other number he'd had under his name. They'd requested this information Wednesday, but here it was Friday already and they hadn't received it. Obtaining phone records always took time. He should have been smart enough to second guess that Jordan had other phones, and requested a warrant earlier.

He took another sip of coffee.

If Jordan had used a burner he'd most likely have tossed it. The only hard evidence they had was that Jordan had built a second remote, or at least made plans for one. But they didn't physically have the remote in their possession and had no clue where it might be. Again, if there was one.

There has to be.

He lumbered toward his desk, surmising that Jordan may have done a runner. He'd waited too long to really lean on him and that was a mistake. If Jordan did run, there was no way to track him. They'd taken his phone, and his car was old. It didn't have tracking software. The only thing Guerrero could do was put out a BOLO and hopefully bring him in that way.

He needed Jordan to crack. He needed to talk to Pete. He needed to find a connection between Jordan and Pete, if there even was one.

What he really needed was a big break.

***

This time Wayne went to Pete. He sat in his Lexus and waited for the gate to fully open before he drove up the drive and parked near the front door. He rang the bell and Pete let him inside.

"My God, man. You're going backwards. Look at you. Look at this place. The gardens are overgrown." He drew his fingers across the round table in the foyer and showed Pete the dust. "Did you fire all the help?"

"I needed to be alone in my house." Pete stared at the floor. He was wearing his pajamas, although he looked like he hadn't slept. He looked gaunt, with bags under his eyes, and disheveled hair.

"That's the last thing you need. Hire them back! Or sell this monstrosity and buy a smaller place. What about Robina?"

"I think she finally left me."

"What?"

"I watched the news last night. She told me not to, but I did it anyway and she got mad."

"You watched the news. You watched the memorial. You heard what some of the people said about you."

"I saw Darius give an interview. I think he knows who I am. I think he always knew. He lied to me."

"I don't know who Darius is, but I'll bet *you* lied to *him*. Who is he anyway? This is the second time I've heard his name."

"What do you mean?"

"I met your therapist, well, your ex-therapist, at the memorial last night. She asked me if I knew who Darius was."

"Why would she do that? I never told her about him."

"Obviously."

"How would she know about him?"

"I think you need to keep seeing her. You were doing so well, and now. Well now." He held his palms out toward Pete. "Have you looked in the mirror? When was the last time you ate?"

"I can't meet with Harmony anymore. Darius said to watch out."

"Darius said for you not to see Harmony?"

"No. He said it was too late. Or, rather, Andrea said it was too late. He didn't mention Andrea's name though. I don't know. I don't know. I'm confused."

"That's an understatement." Wayne took a quick glance around. "I don't suppose you have any coffee made."

"Do you smell any?"

"Get dressed. I'm taking you out to eat. I'm hungry and you need sustenance. No arguing."

Pete looked down at his pajamas. "I'm not hungry."

"You're never hungry. Put food in your mouth, chew, and swallow anyway. I'm not kidding."

Pete turned around and started to trudge to his master suite on the first floor.

"If you aren't back here in ten minutes I'm coming in. And while you're getting dressed, if you won't see Harmony, think who you might see. You have to be in therapy. It's the only way to get you back on your feet."

Pete and Wayne sat in a booth at the restaurant nearest Pete's house, paper plates of food before them. Wayne was halfway through his chicken club. Pete had taken one bite of his hamburger.

"Another." Wayne felt like a nursemaid, but he would do what he had to do. "And pop a couple of those fries in your mouth."

Pete picked up a french fry and ate it.

"There's a good lad. Sheesh! Is it really that hard to keep yourself alive?"

"Sometimes," Pete replied. His eyes strayed and he stared.

"What is it?" Wayne asked.

"Robina. She's sitting over there."

Wayne didn't bother to look. "Is she? She must have followed us. I guess that means she hasn't given up on you."

"No. She wouldn't. I knew she wouldn't."

"Why don't you ask her to join us?"

Pete shook his head. "No. I'll see her back at the house."

"Eat!"

Pete popped another fry in his mouth.

"Have you figured out who you might see instead of Harmony? Or are you going random again? Or do you want me to find a therapist?"

"No. I think I know who to contact."

"All right. That's progress. Who is it?"

"Someone Harmony once said she'd like to consult with about me. I didn't want her to."

"What's the name?"

"Jesse something. She gave me his card so I could check him out if I wanted."

"And did you want?"

"No. I just figured if he was good enough for her, then he must be all right."

"Okay, then. It's settled. You'll contact him. Robina's back. You're going to hire some staff for the house—don't argue. All is right with the world."

"Yeah. Except for Darius lying to me." The slight bit of anger he felt appeared to jar his appetite. He took a hearty bite of the hamburger.

Wayne smiled. "There you go. Get mad, not depressed. Apparently it's good for you."

Pete flashed him a hard look.

"While we're on a roll here, there's something else." Wayne took a business card from his wallet. "I hesitate doing this, but maybe you should talk to this guy."

"What now?" He sounded irritated.

"There you go. Have another fry."

"I'm not ten."

"Are you sure?"

"What is it?"

"In addition to meeting Harmony, I also met a cop at the memorial. He wants to talk to you."

Pete suddenly went pale. "Why? Am I being accused of something new?"

"Don't panic. The answer to your question is no. Did you hear about the murder of Archibald Bent?"

"No. Who is that?"

Wayne was suddenly at a loss for words. He didn't want to bring up anything that might derail Pete's emotional stability any more than it already was. "Maybe we should save this for later." He started to put the card back in the wallet.

"No. You brought it up. I'm feeling pretty strong right now. You know, having eaten my Wheaties and all."

"You're sure?"

Pete nodded.

"This man was killed in a very bizarre way and it was caught on video. Some of it, anyway. It was leaked to the media. And, and . . . Okay, first I need to tell you that he had some sort of vendetta against your sister. A bee in his bonnet, they used to say."

"That's refreshing. At least it wasn't against me for a change."

Wayne smiled. "You are feeling better. Anyway, he'd gone on podcasts and posted nasty stuff on his Facebook page about her. So, of course, when he was murdered, some people said he deserved it and Andrea—or rather her ghost—did him in. Her voice is on the video. It's all very spooky." He paused.

Pete stared at Wayne. "Maybe she did kill him."

Wayne set his jaw. His face clearly said he did not believe Andrea was a ghost and it bothered him Pete did.

"You can discuss that with your next shrink," Wayne said. "But, for your information, the police don't think so."

"Do they think I did it?"

"No. Of course, not. It's an extremely tenuous link, this Archibald, the murder, Andrea, then you. But this detective." He glanced at the card. "Detective Guerrero. He'd like to speak with you. I said I'd tell you. I didn't promise anything else."

Pete held out his hand. Wayne gave him the card.

***

Harmony had a headache, but she met with the two clients she had scheduled for the morning and was grateful when the sessions were over. She still hadn't checked her email or turned on her phone. It was called avoidance. She wasn't ready to hear back from Darius. She wasn't sure she wanted to talk to him.

After the last client left her office, she decided to put on her big girl panties and see if Darius had left a message. Still sitting in her comfortable "interview" chair, she turned on her phone and found that he had not. She checked her emails. Nothing. She thought that was strange and jumped when her cell phone suddenly sang.

"Dr. McKenna," she said.

"Harmony, this is Darius."

Her heart began to pound. "Ah, yes. How are you?" She rolled her eyes. Why had she even asked?

"I'm well, thank you. Are you prepared to meet with me? I have time this afternoon."

Pound. Pound. Pound. What was she so nervous about? The world as she understood it had already been turned upside down. What could this man say that would make it any worse?

"I can do that."

"I live and work in NoHo." He gave her the address. "Shall we say two o'clock?"

"That will work."

"Excellent. *Namaste.*" He hung up.

Harmony sat in her chair, listening to her heartbeat.

Chapter 15

Harmony stood in front of Darius' door and knocked. She could feel her mouth puckering and her body stiffening. Every part of her did not want to meet this man. She absolutely knew he was a fraud, with his culturally-appropriated mode of dress and his peaceful-energy shtick.

Namaste, my ass.

The door opened and there he stood, in a white tunic and loose white cotton pants, beads and chains hanging around his neck.

You look like a flower-power hippie from the sixties. In addition to your psychic super powers, do you travel to and fro in time?

"Welcome," he said with his ritual of praying hands and slight bow. "Please come in."

What, no namaste?

"Thank you," Harmony managed to say as she entered.

He led her to a door and opened it. They went inside. She wasn't in the slightest bit afraid of him, because something told her he wasn't dangerous. But she didn't like him. She didn't like that Peter sought this man's help. He could display a hundred certificates and diplomas on the walls of his office, even one from Harvard. That meant squat. He wasn't a proper therapist. She resented that he had the nerve to counsel people and snow them with his boloney psychic skills.

It's all crap.

"Where would you prefer to sit?"

Harmony looked around. "The love seat, I guess." She walked over and sat down.

He smiled. "Robina's favorite spot."

She felt a chill ravage her blood. Why had he said that? "You've met Robina? Because I haven't."

"No. It's just that when he thinks of her, his eyes go to that spot."

"What?"

"Robina isn't real. You know that."

"No. I don't know that. He mentions her all the time."

"He doesn't talk about her to me. He's tried to remain anonymous and I let him. My approach is to allow the client to work out things as much as he or she can for themselves."

"Uh-huh. So not revealing himself to you is all part of the process." She hoped she didn't sound as sarcastic as she felt.

He merely smiled.

"Why do you say Robina isn't real?" Harmony asked.

"Well, she was. She died."

"Oh, right. You're a psychic medium. Robina's a ghost."

"I didn't say that."

"What then?"

"She is that aspect of his psyche working hard to keep him from killing himself."

Harmony pursed her lips. It felt like he was putting her down.

Didn't *she* know who Robina was? *What* Robina was. Why would she know that? How did *he* know that? How did she know he was right? She didn't. It was probably more of his shtick.

"Well, I didn't come here to talk about Robina."

He gazed at her and said nothing. The pressure was on. She'd called him, although he'd issued an invitation on public television. Without thinking, she picked up a throw pillow that said "Life is an incredible journey" and hugged it to her chest. She took a deep breath. "To be honest, something very strange happened to me, something I'd rather not talk about, but it led me to you."

He was so calm, so confident, it unnerved her. She was in his playpen—that was why. They should have met in her office, she decided.

"Shall we cut to the chase?" he asked.

"Please." She lowered the pillow, but still clung to it.

"Whether you believe there are ghosts or not, and I'm certain you don't, Andrea managed to make herself known to you, just as she makes herself known to me from time to time. She isn't all that powerful. She has a lot to learn as a spirit on the other side. She has amends to make. She is very sorry for what she did, and she is very attached to her brother."

Harmony took a shaky breath. She realized how weak she looked with the pillow on her lap, laid it aside, and cleared her throat. "I don't know anything about all that."

"No. You wouldn't. That's why she wanted you to talk to me."

Silence filled the air. Harmony wanted him to just tell her what he was supposed to tell her so she could get the hell out.

"Andrea is worried about you."

"A worried ghost. Okay."

"Andrea scared her brother away from his last session with you, but now she has indicated to me that it was too little too late. You and Pete are in danger."

Harmony squeezed her lips together and stared Darius in the eye. "Danger. Oh, my. Might you know who this person is we should look out for?"

"I do not. Conversations with Andrea are sporadic and it's not like talking to a living person. I'm dealing with words here and there, symbols, and energy. In other words, I get the gist."

"And hope you're right." It was a barb. Harmony smiled.

"I can tell you I think this person drives a tan Volkswagen bug. However, I do not know that for a fact. Andrea did not say."

"And I don't know anyone who owns a tan Volkswagen bug, so there's that. Okay, then." Harmony rose to her feet. "If that's all, I'll be on my way."

Darius put his hands together in the prayerful position he was so fond of and nodded. He walked with her to the door. She paused at the donation basket. "Do you really make enough to live on doing this?" It was an impertinent question, but he was impertinent claiming to be some sort of psychic expert and charging for it.

For the first time his expression showed displeasure because of her disrespect. "I am certain I charge a lot less than you do seeking to help people. We just have different methods. Good day."

His tone was final. Harmony took her leave. She did not say goodbye. Stabs of guilt pummeled her chest. His words had penetrated her emotional armor. She needn't have been so hostile. They were on the same side. Had she forgotten what happened in the bathroom at Peter's house? Maybe, she thought, I should go back and apologize.

No need.

She froze. That was Darius' voice.

No. Couldn't be.

But it was. She was certain of it. She spun around and pounded on Darius' door. He opened it just as she began to pound a second time.

"What was that?" Harmony asked before he could say or do anything.

"Did you want to come back inside?" Darius asked.

"No! I do not want to come back inside. I want an explanation."

"Then perhaps you could lower your voice."

Harmony was about to tell him she would speak at any level she pleased when she realized she was overreacting. "Sorry. I heard you. I heard you in my head!"

"I sent you a message since you were feeling guilty and already out the door."

"What are you? Some sort of Penn and Teller?"

"Not at all. I merely hoped to put a small chink in your armor with a little trick."

"Then it was a trick."

"Not how you mean. I can, at times, send mental messages to receptive people. Who knew you would be one?"

Harmony could feel anger stirring in her belly.

"No need to get upset," Darius said. "I won't do it again. And you can pretend it never happened. You can keep your armor intact."

She opened her mouth to speak, but nothing came out. Darius closed the door.

***

Pete sat at his desk in the study of his house, cell phone to his ear. Wayne sat across from him, watching his every move. Pete's eyes were closed as if he were blocking out the scary part of a movie. Somehow being unable to see made it easier to call the people he'd fired.

"I would be very grateful if you would return, Pascual. Yes, you and your crew." He listened and nodded. "I understand your first time back will cost more because everything is overgrown now. Everything is a mess." He listened. "Okay, thank you. A week from Tuesday is fine. I understand you are very busy with new customers." He listened again, and his lips took on a small smile. "Of course, if you are too busy, I can hire someone else. My neighbor—" He listened again.

Pascual's voice rose with animation and Wayne could hear what he was saying. "No, no, no, no, no. I can come. We can come. We will be there."

"Tuesday?"

Wayne couldn't hear again. Pascual had lowered his voice.

"This Tuesday or a week from Tuesday?" Pete listened. "This Tuesday. Very good. I will see you then."

Pete hung up and opened his eyes. Wayne leaned in. "You're a sly one. I knew the old Pete was in there somewhere."

"The art of negotiation is a bit like riding a bicycle."

"One never forgets. Now. For Dr. Jesse, whatever his last name is."

Pete looked at Wayne with the eyes of a basset hound begging to be left alone.

"Go on," Wayne said. "You have the card out already. It's right there in front of you. You can do it. I have faith."

Pete tried to stare his business partner down without success.

"Feeling feisty today. I like it. Now call."

Pete looked at the card and punched in the number. A recording answered, "This is Dr. Evans. I will be away from the office until Wednesday. At the tone, please leave your name and number and I will call you back."

Pete hung up.

Wayne frowned.

"Later. I'll call later."

The minute Wayne left the house, Pete started to rip up Jesse's business card. Then he thought better of it and placed it back in the desk.

***

Harmony returned to her favorite Italian restaurant and sat in Richard's section. She'd come early since she'd skipped lunch, and because her visit with Darius left her stomach churning, begging to be fed.

"Just me," she told Richard, and for half a second he looked crestfallen. She smiled. "He does love you in his own small way."

"Did I say anything?" He placed a basket of breadsticks on the table. "Besides, I think it's shameful how he treats you. Always late. I wouldn't have a boyfriend who treated me like that. No matter how good looking he was."

"Sure you wouldn't." Harmony chuckled.

"Well. Not for long, anyway." Richard stuck out his chin. "What can I get you? The usual?"

"I'm driving, so just one glass of my favorite Merlot. And since I'm not waiting for anybody, I'll order . . ." She paused. "You know what? I'll have spaghetti and meatballs. I always loved that when I was a kid."

"Me, too." He wrote it down, but didn't leave. He placed a finger against his cheek and stared at her. "There's something different about you. And I'm not talking spaghetti and meatballs."

"Well, I'm here alone."

"There's that. Have you broken up? You look . . . perturbed. Yes, that's the word for it. Perturbed. What happened? Where is Jesse, anyway?"

"He went out of town to think."

"Ohhh. To think." Richard's eyes narrowed. "That's not good."

Harmony laughed. "Why?"

"It means there's something to think about." Richard punctuated the comment by lowering his head while still eyeing her.

"Maybe we both needed a break from each other. I'm fine with it."

"That's not good either."

"No? Could be you're right. Maybe I should give our relationship some serious thought. That must be what he's doing."

"Hmmm. I'll bring you your wine. I always think better with a glass of red."

He left and Harmony turned her thoughts to Jesse. She realized she didn't care if he was thinking about ending their relationship. She was grateful for how he'd supported her in the hospital and afterward when she came home. But that wasn't love. Well, it became love. She was certain of that. But did she love him now? She didn't know. He'd seemed different, of late. And there was something else. Something nebulous that she never completely understood, but had embraced. From the very beginning she felt as if Jesse fed off her energy. Not in some horrible way that drained her. In a way that actually made her feel good, made her feel needed. It was as if she gave him balance and that helped give her life meaning.

He'd helped her after the encounter with the maniac and she was helping him in return. But she didn't feel that way anymore. The tit for tat, if it ever really existed, was lost. Oh, God. She was circling the drain, over thinking stuff. The issue was simple. Did she love Jesse anymore or not?

Avoiding the answer, she turned her thoughts to ghosts and messages from the beyond, which annoyed her.

"Darius," she said softly. "This is your fault. You got me all discombobulated with your hocus-pocus crap."

Richard set her wine down before her. "Hocus-pocus?"

Harmony felt her face turn red. He'd heard her.

"No need to be embarrassed. I love me a little hocus-pocus," Richard said.

She took a sip of the Merlot. "Yeah? Well, tell me this. Do you believe there are such things as ghosts?"

"You bet your sweet booty I do. I lived with one. And let me tell you, it was no fun."

"You said you loved a bit of hocus-pocus."

"Enchantment, yes. But you can keep the dead people. Mmm-hmmm. No thank you."

He moved to another table and greeted the guests who had just sat down. The place was getting busy. There would be no more small talk with Richard.

Chapter 16

Tears of terror streamed down the naked redhead's cheeks. Her panties were stuffed in her mouth and had been secured with a gag tied at the back of her head. Jesse had covered her mouth this way, not because anybody could hear her scream, but because Jesse didn't want the fuss.

She sat in the middle of Jesse's bedroom, in one of the oak chairs he'd taken from the dining room. Zip ties secured her ankles to the chair legs. One of Jesse's belts strapped her to the chair back. Her wrists were tied behind her with a rag. At the moment she was in resting mode, but sooner or later hysteria would take over and she'd struggle again.

Jesse sat in another of the dining room chairs facing her. He reached across and lovingly brushed aside a lock of hair that had become fixed to her face with the wet of her tears. She jerked her head away.

"Come on, Katie. Let me see those pretty green eyes."

She immediately closed them.

"Okay. Be that way."

Squeals came from the back of her throat as she uselessly tried to jerk free again.

"Here's the thing. I've always wanted to know why I am the way I am. Even as a kid I had all these thoughts and emotions I didn't understand. I liked to hurt people. So it made perfect sense that I would study psychology and become a shrink. I thought all those classes would help me figure myself out. But, you know what? They didn't. I can't tell you why I kill. And I don't know why I don't feel any guilt.

"It's interesting. I once counseled a woman who felt guilty for being the center of attention at her own wedding. I kid you not. The opposite of a bridezilla." He shook his head and chuckled. "Her mother had done a number on her.

"Now me. I could kill twenty people—well, I have killed twenty people, twenty-three to be exact—and it's nothing. It's like breathing the air. I savor it. I enjoy it. I keep little mementos to remember . . . ah!"

He raised a finger, stood, and picked up his cell phone lying on the dresser. "I haven't had this thing on all day. I should have had it ready." He pressed a button, swiped, put in his password, and waited as the phone went through the process of firing up. "Bear with me here."

Katie's tears continued to flow as she hiccupped deep in her chest.

"Come on. Come on. Okay." He moved in front of Katie. "Look at me." She kept her head averted. He took hold of her chin and jerked her face to where he wanted. "I can get rough," he asserted. She kept her head where he'd placed it but wouldn't look at him. He took a picture with the phone. He checked it. "It'll do." He put the phone back on the dresser and sat.

"Now where was I? Guilt. I don't have any. I've tried to determine if it's because of anything my mother or father did. Is it something I learned? I don't know. After I tell you this, see what you think.

"My father had lots of affairs. He traveled a lot. So yeah, one-night stands. But he'd have affairs that would last for months. Nothing my mother ever said or did made him stop. And she did plenty. Smashed windshields. Scratched up cars. She left a birthday present on one woman's porch that had a snake in it. A harmless snake, but some people have phobias. I'm pretty sure this woman did. Neither of my parents ever killed anybody, though. Not that I know of.

"Now if you look at serial killers, and I've analyzed plenty of them, you'll see a lot of child abuse and ice-cold mothers with no heart. They even try to say Ted Bundy finding out that his older sister was actually his birth mother helped shape him into what he was. But Jack Nicholson's sister turned out to be his mother and he became an actor, not a murderer. So, I don't know.

"I certainly never got the belt. My father wasn't a drunk. I don't know if you'd call my mother cold. I know she was warmer to my brother. She liked him best. I did sort of hate her for it. Mostly I hated him. But we won't go there."

He sighed and looked at Katie, which caused her to squirm. He chuckled.

"Once I discovered the joy of killing I became a cheerful, prolific murderer. The highs are indescribable when you kill someone right. And, here's another interesting fact, I like to experiment. Kill in different ways. My last experiment wasn't all that satisfying, I must admit. Did you hear about the man beheaded with a guillotine?"

Katie began to squeal in short bursts.

"Yeah. That was me. I was irritated because my girlfriend had become disloyal. I wanted to upset her by driving the object of her affection, this man named Pete, crazy. She'd been mentioning him in her sleep for weeks. So when this opportunity came up, I thought, what an original way to kill someone. I could record the murder, create the illusion that Pete's sister committed it—she's supposed to be a ghost—and then have the video leaked to the press. Without going into the psychology of it, Pete should have gone bonkers. The problem is I have no idea if Pete ever even saw the video. He quit seeing my girlfriend. She's his therapist. Was his therapist. So it appears to have been all for naught. I will say it was fun being creative and all, but I kind of prefer my kills to be up close and personal. Pulling on a cord and having a blade slice off someone's head didn't quite do it for me. I did rather enjoy picking the old guy up and slamming him onto the guillotine, then strapping him down. Watching him struggle was pretty good."

Jesse's eyes slid downward as he remembered.

"Harmony. Harmony. Harmony," he murmured. "What happened to us?"

He looked at Katie. "I quit killing for close to six years because of her. I have no idea why. She cast a spell on me. And then she broke it." He lifted his hands, put his fingers together and spread them apart as if he were a magician who'd made something disappear. "Poof!"

Jesse stared down at the area rug on the bedroom floor. "And you know what? I'm sad about that. She's no longer of use to me. My dreams of normalcy have flown out the window. Wham, bam, thank you ma'am. But I don't want to kill her. I want to torture her. Emotionally, I mean. And I want to kill him. Oh yes. That would be a pleasure. I just have to decide when and how. I like knives. I have quite the collection. And I've been practicing. You know, firing them off and hitting my target. I'm already proficient at plunging."

He demonstrated, thrusting an invisible knife in the air.

"I just need to pick my moment."

He turned his gaze back to Katie. "Thank you so much for listening to me. I don't see therapists myself. It's a little difficult to share my true thoughts with others. And anyway, I've accepted what I am so there's no point."

His eyes bored into her and she began to thrash about, rocking the chair from side to side in a frenzy. He watched, fascinated. He shook his head, marveling.

"Expending all that energy when you know it won't do any good."

The chair—with Katie—fell on its side.

"Now look what you've done." Jesse stood up and righted the chair as if it weighed nothing.

He moved behind her.

"Did I tell you how much I like the tattoo on your hand?" He began to softly stroke her hair with his palms and all of his fingers. She jerked her head this way, then that, emitting muffled cries the entire time. "Really nice work. I don't have a tattoo myself. It would make me too easy to identify should someone see it at an inopportune moment. You know what I mean?"

He slid one hand down to her chin and stepped to the side of the chair. The other hand he placed on her crown. "Yeah. A really sweet tattoo. What I'd call nice and clean."

In a flash he pushed her chin away from him, snapping the head toward him and downward with the hand on her crown. Katie's neck cracked and broke. She fell silent.

"Well. That was quick," Jesse said. *Maybe too quick. But the last thing I needed was a bloody mess on my bedroom floor.*

He picked up his phone and took a shot of dead Katie.

"Another one for the record books."

Jesse spent the next few hours cleaning up. He sent the pictures to his printer and made copies for his trophy room. He threw Katie in a wheelbarrow, along with her clothing, and transported her to the mine that way. He changed the sheets on his bed and wiped fingerprint evidence away from every place he thought she had been, not that he believed anyone would come looking.

By the time he dropped into bed it was three in the morning. Exhausted, he almost didn't bother to check his phone. Certainly there would be texts from Harmony and there were. Not as many as he thought there might be. But a couple. When was he coming home? She thought they should talk.

Yada, yada, yada.

He sent back a quick response that he wasn't sure. Maybe tomorrow. He thought they should talk as well. About to put the phone on the night stand and plug it in to keep its charge, he caught sight of a missed call. From Pete Ashton! He checked and there was no message, but his phone had identified him. Pete apparently didn't call anonymously. How fortunate! Jesse now had the perfect reason to call Pete and ask him what he needed. A new therapist perhaps?

Jesse rubbed his hands together in glee. He'd call him. Oh boy, would he. Obviously, not right now, but waiting for morning was going to be tough.

Or so he thought. He actually slept like a baby.

Chapter 17

When Detective Guerrero arrived at work, he found Jordan's cell phone data on his desk. It went back four months and was for the number he'd previously used with the phone he'd gotten rid of. Somewhere in the mishmash of numbers should be this Dr. J. The data didn't give the name of the person Jordan had called. The numbers would have to be checked out. Or, someone could just start calling and see who answered. Feeling a bit petulant because of the lack of progress he'd made on the case, and because he'd been so stupid as to not do a full-court press on Jordan before he disappeared, and because Jordan had vanished like a fart in the wind—as warden Norten said in *Shawshank Redemption*, one of Guerrero's favorite movies—Guerrero called the first number and got the voice mail for Little Caesar's.

"Pizza," he grumbled as he clicked off. *Slow and steady wins the race*, he reminded himself. *Be the tortoise, not the hare.*

The detective stood up and stretched his back. Pete Ashton hadn't contacted him as he'd hoped, but he really wasn't certain there was a connection that would help. The best he could do was visit Mrs. Lyman again and try to jog her memory about Dr. J. Also, it could be that she knew where Jordan was and had decided to help shield him from the police. He would press her about this. He'd have Berry work on the phone list while he was out.

Guerrero was about to stick his arms into his jacket when he heard his name. "Donato, Mrs. Lyman is here to see you."

Guerrero turned around. A young deputy was walking away, leaving Jordan's mother to fend for herself. The woman was sober and fidgeting with her hands. Guerrero motioned to the chair on the opposite side of his desk and she sat, looking very small and sad.

"Funny thing," Guerrero said. "I was just leaving to come see you. Any word from Jordan?"

She shook her head and removed a tissue from her pocketbook. She dabbed at her eyes, which Guerrero now saw were red. "I'm frightened, detective."

"I see that. You think something happened to your son?"

She nodded. "He doesn't do this. He doesn't disappear. He's a homebody. He likes his room in the garage. He likes to tinker and make things. He's all I have. He's a good son. He does my grocery shopping."

This version was different than the way she'd talked about Jordan the other night when she'd been drinking. It was true, however. People had many facets to them.

"That's nice," Guerrero assured her. "The other night you told me he lied to you. You said he was off to see this Dr. J. You don't believe that's the case?"

"I don't know." A tear trickled from one eye and she mopped it with the tissue. "I get mad at him sometimes. But that's normal, isn't it? He hates that I drink. Oh, I'm aware of how bad I can be. I don't think that's why he left me, though. It's why he made up a room in the garage."

"Is that why he started seeing a therapist?"

"No. No. That was something else. He killed the neighbor's cat and that's a warning sign, isn't it?" The tears really flowed now. "I wanted him to talk to someone. The neighbor was very upset. Their daughter was very upset. They accused Jordan, but they had no proof. I knew he'd probably done it. He'd killed a cat before, so it made sense that he'd killed their cat. I shouldn't have complained about my roses and the smell. See? Jordan was thinking of me. He is a good son."

This information piqued the old cop's interest. Killing animals was a huge red flag. He was more convinced than ever that Jordan was the key to solving this murder.

"I need to find Jordan."

"That's why I'm here. I want you to find him. I didn't call because he took my phone. Why would he take my phone and not come home? Something's wrong. A mother knows these things."

The woman wouldn't be this upset if he just did a runner. Well, he supposed she could be, but it was more likely she thought something bad had happened to him. "Mrs. Lyman. If Jordan merely ran off, would he have told you he was going to do that?"

"No. But he would have called after he left to tell me he was fine." She fiddled with the tissue in her hands.

Guerrero felt a stab to his gut. He thought something bad had happened to Jordan as well. This accomplice, possibly Dr. J, could have thought Jordan was a problem and done something about it. The fact that Jordan had swiped his mother's phone might be helpful if he'd kept it on, and why wouldn't he? They could obtain data on Mrs. Lyman's phone that would tell Guerrero where he'd gone.

"All right. If you give permission to your phone carrier to release your phone's records, we won't need to get a warrant and we should be able to see where Jordan went. At least the general vicinity. Does that sound like a plan to you?"

She nodded. "Where do I sign?"

Guerrero smiled. "A call will do."

***

Harmony walked through the women's clothing section of Nordstom's, stopping to admire a plaid blazer appropriate for work or play. She was only shopping to distract herself and lost interest in the blazer immediately.

She was off her game and she knew it. Messages from ghosts. The idea that there were ghosts! And now a spiritual guru who seemed to know more about Peter than she did. Plus, Jesse was acting weird. He'd become inconsiderate, secretive, and elusive—disappearing for days. She was more convinced than ever that they should break up. Everything was off-kilter. Her confidence had been undermined. She needed a therapist, or at the very least a sounding board. That had been Jesse's role in her life, and she couldn't turn to him.

Darius.

Oh, no. No. No. No. No. No. She wasn't going down that road. That road was for fools.

Is Peter a fool?

Yes! There was no way she was going to seek the help of someone like Darius, a self-appointed expert in the field of mumbo jumbo.

What about your encounter with Andrea?

Shut up.

What about hearing Darius' voice in your head?

I said, shut up.

Who are you talking to?

I'm talking to myself. I'm not crazy.

I didn't say you were, but it wouldn't hurt to talk to the man. I mean, what are you afraid of?

"Grrrrr!" Harmony looked over and saw a pretty twenty-something woman glance her way. "Sorry," Harmony said.

"Prices these days," the pretty woman said. "It sure stretches my paycheck. But this is the only place I shop."

Harmony grabbed the blazer from the rack, then found a camisole. A flattering, black, halter-neck jumpsuit caught her eye even though she couldn't think of a place to wear it. She needed some sexy pieces to balance the practical blazer. She needed to connect with old friends or make some new ones. She'd allowed Jesse to become her life. He hadn't demanded it. She'd never felt coerced, but somehow it had happened just the same. Her life needed to change. She needed to feel good about herself. She needed . . . she needed . . .

She needed to talk to Darius. She sighed, deflated. She had to face it. He knew things. If he freaked her out, she could run out the door. Yes. She could always do that.

She took her finds to the cashier without even trying them on.

***

Pete answered his cell phone even though the caller ID clearly read Dr. Evans. He was still in bed at eleven-forty in the morning, head buried in the pillow. Yesterday, with Wayne, he'd felt strong. Today, not so much. And Robina was starting to make herself scarce. He didn't like that.

"Hello."

"Peter! How are you? This is Dr. Evans. My caller ID alerted me to your call even though you didn't leave a message. What can I do for you?"

"Uh." Pete said nothing for a full fifteen seconds. "I don't know. Probably nothing." He turned on his back and threw an arm over his eyes.

"That sounds rather bleak. Why did you call?"

Another pause, but shorter. "I was encouraged to."

"Oh? May I ask by whom?"

"You can ask." Pete didn't give him an answer. "I was pressured into calling you."

"You were."

"Yes. But I think right now I want to be left alone. Allowed to rot, if you will."

"Now, that does make it sound as if you need my help."

"Let's leave it at this. If I need you, I'll call you." Pete hung up. He didn't like being rude, especially after experiencing the cutting remarks he received from strangers who didn't know what the hell they were talking about. He definitely didn't want to be like one of them. He'd always been a thoughtful person, and he'd been thoughtful toward his sister. Why she suddenly decided he'd turned against her and done what she did . . .

He felt that draining mixture of sorrow, anger, and fear fill his stomach, mind, and chest. He turned on his side, reached for the bedside table, and dropped the phone. Then he hugged the pillow as he curled into a fetal position. Guilt filled every cell of his body. If he'd been clearer with Andrea that he intended to help her reignite her career, all those people wouldn't have died. Judging from Andrea's legion of fans who attacked him at every turn, she'd probably be back on top right now and all would be well with the world.

He started to cry when he felt Robina's hand on his shoulder. She was back. Oh, it felt so good for her to be back.

"Go ahead and sleep, if that's what you need. I'm here."

"Don't leave me," he said. "I have this awful feeling something terrible is going to happen."

"Then you might want to consider calling Dr. McKenna. She seemed to be helping you make progress. I think you need her."

Tears wet Pete's pillowcase.

Robina continued. "What was it Darius said? Something about it being too late anyway?"

"Yeah." Pete wiped his eyes. "He said it was too late."

"So? Do you want to call her?"

Pete nodded. The idea of talking to Dr. McKenna comforted him. He drifted off to sleep.

***

Jesse fumed. Maneuvering Pete Ashton into his orbit might not be as simple as it first appeared to be. But he'd find a way, he assured himself. It was time to leave Scarlett and go back to Sherman Oaks. First, he would mend fences with Harmony, get that relationship back on track. Then, as he worked with Pete and made him worse, not better, he'd let Harmony see his handiwork. She wouldn't know he'd done it on purpose. He'd merely throw up his hands about how bad things had gotten for Pete—Peter—and he'd make sure she knew he thought it was her fault.

He picked up his phone. No texts from Harmony. He'd tell her he was back once he was home. He was about to put the phone in his pocket when a news feed caught his eye. The lead story was a local one. Someone named Katie was seen getting into a Volkswagen bug in Big Bear and had not come home. No big deal, except she was from out of town and was supposed to catch a plane and had reassured her cousin that she wouldn't stay out all night.

"Jesus Christ!" Jesse said, a sense of panic erupting all over his body. He decided it was best not to drive the Volkswagen home, just in case some diligent San Bernardino county sheriff decided to stop him and take his information merely because he was in the bug. He'd drive the Chevy Colorado instead.

Needing little in the way of preparation, Jesse was ready in a flash. He manually opened the garage door, tossed his overnight bag into the truck, and drove out. With the motor running, he climbed out and closed the garage. "I should get that fixed," he mumbled as he climbed back into the vehicle. He drove down the gravel drive to the gate and pressed the opener he kept in the glove compartment. As he drove onto the dirt road, a baby-blue Dodge pickup that had seen better days rolled up and blocked his path. A man in his late fifties sporting a short gray beard, plastic-rimmed glasses, and a cowboy hat leaned out the driver's side window. He motioned for Jesse to roll his window down, which Jesse did.

"Howdy. Might you be my seldom-seen neighbor, Jesse Evans?"

Jesse pressed the button to close the gate. He had no clue who the man was. "If you live nearby, I guess I am."

"I'm Al. Live down the road a piece." He gestured with his thumb. "Hawkeye didn't think you'd mind if I borrowed your propane tank. Got a barbecue coming up and mine's shot. Literally shot. I got me some teenage boys, grandkids, you know. And sometimes I think all they do is figure out ways to destroy my stuff." He chuckled. "You've heard'a chip off the old block? That'd be them. You're welcome to join us for the barbecue. Hawkeye was intendin' to come. But I sure need . . ."

"Uh, yeah," Jesse said, wanting to get away from this old codger as quickly as he could. "I remember Hawkeye mentioning the tank, but he said he couldn't find it and I don't know where it could have gone." Jesse wiped the top of his lip. "He didn't give you a call?"

"I'm sure he said it was here. Is he home?"

"I haven't seen him."

"Well, shucks. I've been puttin' off buying a new one. You know how that goes. We don't barbecue all that much, but this is sort of a special occasion. You sure Hawkeye's not here?"

"I'm sure."

"Hmmm. He should'a called me or somethin'." Al looked perplexed.

Jesse figured if he didn't get going his neighbor would keep him here all day.

"Look, I've got to head out. It was nice meeting you and all that. But could you move your truck?"

Al laughed. "Sure thing. Didn't mean to corral you in like that. I wasn't thinking. You headin' back home down the hill?"

"I am." *Not that it's any of you business.* "And I'd like to get a move on."

"Okay." Al ducked back into the cab and put the Dodge in reverse. He steered to the side of the road.

Jesse waved and stomped on the gas. His tires kicked up a load of dust as he sped away, headed for another dirt path that would dump him onto the paved highway. He checked the rearview mirror. Al and his truck were fast becoming a speck in the road.

"You can go on home now, you old coot. There's no one's ear left to chew on." Jesse turned and Al became a memory.

* * *

Once his part-time neighbor was out of sight, Al smacked his lips together. "That Jesse makes no sense," he said aloud, used to having his Irish Setter, Blarney, by his side. Sadly his companion had died not long after New Year's. He looked up at the blue sky as he mulled things through. He knew bullshit when he heard it. Hawkeye would have called if that propane tank was missing. More than likely this Jesse was a skinflint, or just couldn't be bothered. And how could Hawkeye be gone if Jesse had the truck? That was how Hawkeye got around. Jesse's story didn't add up.

He and Hawkeye had become good friends. He'd given Al the gate code months ago. He needed to check the garage for himself. He rolled the truck up to the gate and punched in the code.

Chapter 18

Detective Guerrero came home with Jordan's cell records because Berry was a dumbass. The disinterested detective had been poached by Detective Harris to help with a murder that was fresher than Archibald's, so he had turned over the task of researching Jordan's calls to a green-as-grass deputy who hadn't done a thing. Guerrero would have to review them that night if he wanted to make any progress. He wouldn't get Mrs. Lyman's cell records until tomorrow afternoon at the earliest.

Guerrero spread Jordan's phone records out on the kitchen table. He looked for numbers that had been called several times and circled those to check first. He opened his computer and found a reverse look-up site. He'd asked, but he wasn't going to wait for the phone company to come through with what number belonged to whom. It was time for full speed ahead.

***

Standing in her bedroom, Harmony stepped into the black halter jumpsuit and was pleased to find it fit like a glove. Her skin might be scarred, but no one could fault her for not maintaining an eye-catching figure, even though she tended to dress conservatively so as not to attract attention. Jesse had encouraged it, and she'd let him get away with it! Red flags dotted their relationship and she'd ignored them.

She removed the jumpsuit and tossed the black camisole over her head. She stroked the silk and lace fabric and allowed herself to acknowledge that she was an attractive woman with the needs of someone still young and vital. Jesse no longer met those needs. She didn't love him, at least not the way she had, and she didn't believe he loved her. They were in the midst of the swan song of a once hot and romantic relationship. She could now concede that he disrespected her in more ways than one. Late for dates without adequate explanations, often telling her it was no big deal. Encouraging her to cut ties with any friend who wanted to do things without him. And what about the dog she'd found, scared and skinny, looking for a home? Harmony had taken in the mutt over Jesse's protests—it was her house, not his. Why should Jesse get to decide? She'd named the little thing Harpo because he never barked. When the dog suddenly went missing, Jesse insisted she must have left the gate open and he'd run away. She gave Jesse the benefit of the doubt, but part of her wondered if he hadn't taken Harpo to the pound. Although she'd checked the pound and never found him. Also, what about not letting her know she revealed things in her sleep, things he shouldn't hear? How long had that been going on?

He'd been snarky of late and secretive. She didn't like it. Something was wrong. Their relationship was over. Maybe she would tell him they could remain friends, but she didn't even want that. And, she didn't want Jesse showing up in the middle of the night thinking they could be friends with benefits. That wasn't happening. She would change the locks.

As for Peter, she no longer wanted to be his therapist. She cared too deeply for him. She had not technically crossed a line, but as Jesse put it, she had emotionally crossed one. She was going to call him and confess that that was the case. She'd agree they should no long have any contact.

Her cell sang. She checked it. Jesse had called her earlier and texted her. This was him again. She decided to answer or else he might come knocking on her door.

"Hi," she said. "Your messages said you're back. Did you accomplish what you set out to accomplish?"

"I did, I think. I missed you. Would this be a good time to come over?"

"Uh, not really. I'm not home," she lied. Her heart began to pound and she wondered if Jesse could hear it. "Do you think we might have lunch tomorrow?"

"Tomorrow. Of course."

"Good. I think we need to talk."

"So do I," responded Jesse. "One o'clock at the Brewing Company?"

"I'll be there." She wanted to tell him to not be late because she wasn't going to wait for him anymore, but thought better of it.

They hung up without either of them saying the "L" word.

Jesse stared out the window of his Dodge Challenger Demon at Harmony's house. Her car was in the driveway and the lights were on. She was home. She'd lied to him and he did not take kindly to that. Part of him wanted to march up to her door and use the key, but he maintained control. Sparking an argument was not in his plans. He wanted to finesse Harmony. He wanted her to believe he cared and that he desperately needed her. That seemed to be her Achilles heel, the deep-seated desire to help the vulnerable. Like that dumb dog. And as far as humans went, no one was more vulnerable than Pete. Jesse was going to do his best to compete with that, and doing so didn't include being bold enough to walk into her house unannounced. Not now. Not this time.

He started the motor of the Challenger, aware that it was loud. He sped off before—on the off-chance—Harmony checked out the window.

Harmony didn't need to look out the window to recognize the sound of Jesse's car. She'd been in the passenger seat many times when he'd fired up the beast. Was he stalking her now? This was crazy.

She immediately went online to find a 24-hour locksmith, cost be damned. It wasn't all that late. Only eight o'clock. The person who answered the phone said she could be at the house in twenty minutes, not a problem. In the meantime, she was going to make that call to Peter. It took her ten minutes to build up the courage, but she finally managed it.

To her surprise, he answered. "Hello, Dr. McKenna."

"Peter. Oh, God. I was going to leave a message."

"I'm sorry I've ignored all your calls. That was rude."

Harmony swallowed, her blood pulsing a little too fast.

"I had reason to believe we shouldn't be in contact," Peter continued.

"Yes. Yes. I totally understood. Understand." Why was she feeling so weak in the throat? She found it difficult to talk. "When a client believes—"

"No. It was Andrea. She thought we shouldn't see each other. But I've come to learn that . . ." It was his turn to swallow. "Come to learn that . . . well, never mind. I was better when you were my therapist. I've been slipping and . . . and . . . well, I discussed it with Robina and I want to come back."

"Robina wants you to come back."

"I want to come back."

Harmony closed her eyes and breathed deeply. She wanted to question him about Robina. Did he physically see her? Was she all in his mind? Did he know that she was some sort of figment, or was Darius full of it? If she started asking questions it could be construed as acting like his therapist and no matter the progress he was asserting, she needed to let him go.

"Peter," she began. "I know you need more therapy and I was truly honored to see that you made great strides under my care. But if I'm being brutally honest, I think I've developed feelings for you that are unethical. They aren't healthy."

"Aren't healthy for whom? Me?" He paused. "Or you?"

"I don't know. I honestly don't. I just can't do anything that could jeopardize your wellness."

Peter was quiet. Harmony felt sick to her stomach. Every part of her ached to see him, to help him, to comfort him. He needed her, and apparently she needed him, or, dare she accept it, wanted him. But she refused to bond with Peter any further. She wasn't the only one who could counsel him. There were many qualified psychologists in the Los Angeles area. She had to let go.

"Can I come see you?" he said very softly.

"What?" Harmony blinked. Had she heard him right? Did he mean it the way it sounded?

"I want to see you," he said.

"I just told you that . . ." She cleared her throat. "That isn't a good idea. I wish you the best. Your mental health is what matters. It really is paramount. Please find someone who can help you, who . . ." She hated saying the next part out loud, but honesty was the correct policy. "Someone who isn't emotionally attached. That is your best course of action, Peter."

She hung up. Tears warmed her eyes. She felt like someone about to board a plane, saying goodbye to a loved one forever. It hurt. It cut like a blade.

She collapsed onto the bed and might have started crying, but then the doorbell rang. The locksmith had arrived and she was grateful for the interruption.

After the locks were changed—front door, back door, garage door to the backyard, and garage door to the house—she changed the security code to the backyard gate. Finally, Harmony decided she could relax. Tomorrow would be another trying day, meeting with Jesse and breaking up with him, but she could do it. She'd hold up. The truth was, she doubted it would be as tough as letting go of Peter. That had been the real challenge.

In keeping with her resolution to free herself of the shackles she'd allowed herself to take on, Harmony decided to skinny dip in her above-ground hot tub. It wasn't as daring as it sounded. The backyard was fenced, as was the hot tub area. Between the many trees growing around the perimeter and the location of the spa, no one would see her.

Harmony exited the house in a short terry robe with flip-flops on her feet. The full moon had been the night before, so technically it wasn't as brilliant, but it still beamed brightly. She crossed the patio to the spa, carrying a towel, a glass of Chardonnay, and a snack-size bag of chips. She put them down on the deck, removed the cover from the spa, and checked the temperature. It was what she considered comfortable, one-hundred degrees. Harmony flipped a switch and the bubbles began to churn. She shed the robe and the shoes and climbed two stair steps so she could get in. With a satisfied sigh, she lowered herself into the water.

In this moment, she wouldn't let her mind chew on any of the issues in her life. She would relax and enjoy. She reached over, grabbed the wine and took a sip. It was cold and not too dry nor too sweet. When she finished with it, she would get out and go to bed. She put the wine glass on the deck, leaned back and closed her eyes. She stretched out her hands and felt the bubbles surface though her fingers. It was amazing how something as simple as sitting in a tub of bubbling water could be so soothing to her soul.

It was—until the sound of the gate opening and closing caused her eyes to open. Someone was coming. She heard their footsteps. How in the world could Jesse know the code to the gate? She wanted to scream. He was intruding. This was her time. Her getaway. He'd had his. He'd left town for days. For a second she thought about rushing out of the hot tub and grabbing her robe, but she'd waited too long. All she could do was stay well below the bubbles to protect what little privacy she had in the situation. She looked up at the person who had stepped onto the deck.

"Peter," her voice a mere whisper. She noted that his hair was cut, and gauntness had returned to his face.

He looked at her sheepishly. Then he turned and sat with his back to her on the edge of the spa. "I, um. I wanted to see you."

"How did you know where I lived? How did you get through the gate? When did you cut your hair?"

"You noticed."

"Of course."

"Do you like it?"

"Yes. What about the rest of my questions?"

"You probably wouldn't believe me."

"Try me." She wasn't angry—only extremely curious. And, if she was completely honest, happy to see him.

"Well, I learned where you lived a long time ago, although I never once dared to drive by."

"I suppose that's a point in your favor. And the gate?"

"I don't know. The number for the code sort of came into my head."

"Was it a voice?"

"Kind of."

"Did it sound like Darius?"

Pete looked at her over his shoulder, surprised. "You know about Darius?"

"I've met Darius." She dipped lower to make sure she stayed beneath the obscuring bubbles and he turned away again. "I met Darius because of your sister," she said. "She found a way to tell me to seek him out."

"Then you believe me about her. I was never sure."

"I don't know what I believe. Not anymore."

He turned to face her full on. She dipped lower in the water as they looked into each other's eyes. She felt bashful, sitting in a tub of whirring water, naked as a newborn. But she also felt good. She was camouflaged enough, and she was with someone she knew was thoughtful and kind. If she told him to leave, she was certain he would.

Pete turned away again and laughed. "I feel wonderful!"

"You do?" Harmony reached for the wine.

He nodded. "You're not my therapist anymore."

"Nope."

"That means we can be friends."

Harmony took a sip from the wine glass. It seemed to her she was walking a fine line. "I think we can."

"More than friends?" he said.

Harmony knew how she felt, but she wasn't sure that it was healthy for Peter to be enamored of her. How genuine was it? Was it that old bugaboo of transference?

"No," Harmony said. "We can be friends. We can have conversations, but it can't be more than that."

She saw his shoulders wilt. "I'll take what I can get," he said softly.

"I need to ask you something," Harmony said. "Would you tell me about Robina?"

He glanced over his shoulder. "Robina was my girlfriend."

"Was? Then, uh, you do know . . ."

"That when I see her she isn't really there? I didn't for a long time. Not for years, when I was at my worst. She was killed in the fire."

"Oh my God," Harmony said quietly.

"I didn't know at first. Wayne kept it from me. He thought it would push me over the edge and it might have. I never sought out a list of the victims. I guess I wanted to stick my head in the sand and keep it there." He paused. "And then one day, quite by accident, I saw a list, along with headshots of the people who died. And there she was. There was my beautiful Robina."

"So you pretended?"

"No. I still saw her, plain as day. I thought she was a ghost, but she didn't act like a ghost. Not that I knew how a ghost should act. Well, I knew how Andrea acted. But, I figured that if every human being is different, ghosts were different, too. I didn't like the idea that she was stuck here and I told her she should go. Go to the light, isn't that what people say? Anyway, she told me not to worry. She wasn't stuck anywhere. After a while, I began to realize that Robina was a part of me. An important, life-giving part of me. I accepted it. I needed it. But lately she's been absent more than she's been present and I'm not sure why that is. Maybe because I'm getting better? Because I don't need her as much. What do you think?"

"It's possible."

The jets shut off and the bubbles slowed to a ripple. Peter politely turned his back. "I think that's my cue," he said.

Harmony watched him stand up.

"Until next time?" he asked rhetorically.

"Until," was all she managed to eke from her mouth. He ambled toward the gate. It crossed her mind that she could tell him it was all right. Just let her put on her robe and he could stay. But she didn't do that. She knew it wouldn't be right. When she heard him exit and the gate clang shut, she picked up the wine and downed it.

Chapter 19

"If you get well—I mean, truly well—then I believe you have a chance for a proper relationship with Harmony," Robina said. "And you won't need me anymore."

Pete brushed his teeth as he looked at Robina in the dressing room mirror and thought about his encounter with Harmony last night. He didn't believe his affection for her was transference. She was the type of person he could love and respect. He had to admit he didn't know her, not really. He didn't know her story, where she was raised, if she had siblings. All that stuff. She had kept their sessions about him. She did say that she'd become a therapist because of the encouragement of a very caring person after she'd nearly been killed. That was the therapist she'd recommended to him, Dr. Evans.

Pete smiled at Robina. He turned to look at her straight on and she was gone. He decided to call this Evans doctor. He went to his office, where he'd left the business card. The doctor answered on the second ring.

Jesse had a charming smile, but when he grinned, which was what he was doing now, he looked predatory. The grin included a frightening glint in his eye and a wolfish snarl about the corners of his mouth. His teeth gleamed as he spoke on the phone. "Peter! You might not believe this, but I was just thinking about you, hoping you would call, thinking I might call you if you didn't. When would you like to come in?"

"Whenever you have an opening. I think I'm ready."

"How about today? I can fit you in at eleven."

"Okay," Pete said. "Where?"

Jesse gave him the address. He hung up and his grin stretched wider, from Los Angeles to Chicago.

***

After combing through Jordan's phone records, Detective Guerrero had come up with two doctors. One was a dentist, a Dr. Johnson. The other was a psychologist named Dr. Jesse Evans. The latter, of course, was Dr. J. He decided he needed to know more about this person of interest before he spoke to him and poached Detective Hernandez to help him. She was more than happy to dig in.

"I'd like to know everything you can find out about this man," Guerrero told her. "Where he lives. Who his friends are. If you can find any of his former clients, that would be a big plus. See if he has any black marks on Yelp. That sort of thing. Exes oftentimes like to share the dirt. Not that this guy is dirty. I may be clutching at straws."

"Gotcha," she said, and she started to clack off in her heels.

"Haven't you broken those in yet?"

"Different shade of red."

Guerrero sighed. Where was that tracking information on Lyman's cell phone? He was tired of waiting. Right now impatience would be his friend. He made a call and learned that the information he wanted had "just arrived."

"Uh-huh," he responded. "Well, get it to me!"

***

Pete sat across from Jesse in Jesse's office and felt prickly and uncomfortable. He was used to Harmony's office with the natural light, live plants, and not too many plaques on the wall. Her office had been inviting, soothing, and reassuring. Jesse's space felt clinical and in-your-face. He counted nineteen framed degrees and awards on the wall behind the doctor so that they were in Pete's line of sight. Did the man have a complex? It seemed like he was trying too hard.

A fly buzzed past Pete's ear and landed on his hand. He looked at it, but didn't shoo it away. What had Anthony Perkins said at the end of the movie *Psycho*? *See I won't even hurt a fly?* Yeah. That was it. Something in Pete wouldn't put it past this doctor to have turned that fly loose just to see what his clients did, even though the suggestion was ridiculous. He stopped looking at the fly and turned his gaze on Dr. Evans. Harmony had recommended Dr. Evans and he trusted her, so he'd do his best to remain open-minded, although at the moment he was silent. He was tired of the narrative, of his story, of everything. He didn't feel like starting over with someone new and explaining it all again. He sighed. If it weren't for his desire to prove to Harmony that he was well, he would walk out the door.

"I can see that you're ready to bolt," Dr. Evans said.

Pete took an unsteady breath. "Am I that transparent?"

"Not at all. I've been doing this a long time and I know the signs. You don't want to repeat yourself for the millionth time. Would that be a fair statement?"

Pete nodded.

"Maybe I can make things easier for you by speeding up the process. Would that be agreeable with you?"

Pete shrugged. This guy was the doctor. He was supposed to know what was best. Why ask him?

"Okay," Dr. Evans said. "Let me just say that I know who you are. I know about your nightclub and what happened to you. I know about your sister."

"Do you know she's a ghost?"

Dr. Evans chuckled, apparently surprised by Pete's sudden response. "I've seen the rumors her fans like to post online."

"No. I mean, do you know she's a ghost? Because she is. Literally."

"Ah. No, I do not know that. Perhaps we should start there." There was something patronizing in his tone.

Harmony had never tried to squash his belief in Andrea the ghost. She'd helped him cope with what he saw. She might have thought it was a hallucination, but she never said anything derogatory about it. She wasn't condescending. Lots of people believed in ghosts. It didn't make them crazy. He certainly wasn't crazy because he believed.

"What do you think about those rumors?" Dr. Evans asked.

"I try to avoid them."

"Why is that?"

"Because it isn't something I can control. And anyway, never mind about Andrea."

"No. I think we should explore this. Your sister's actions had a great impact on your life. If you believe her spirit is still hanging around, that's important."

Pete said nothing. Of course it was important, because she *was* around.

"Did you see the video of Archibald Bent's murder?"

"No."

"A lot of people think it's a video of your sister's ghost committing—"

"I thought you didn't believe in ghosts."

"I didn't say I believed it was her."

Pete thought he caught a flash of anger cross the doctor's face before he recovered with a smile.

"What I'm saying is, other people believe it. Her laugh was caught on the video. And there's audio of her voice."

Pete shrugged.

"Would it upset you to watch it?"

"Of course it would upset me. Not because of Andrea, but because it's a recording of an actual murder. Are you suggesting I should see it?"

The doctor's response was measured. "No," he finally said. The doctor wiped his upper lip and allowed a whispered sigh. "I think you're a lot stronger than Harmony, uh, Dr. McKenna gave you credit."

Pete frowned. He was stronger, thanks to her. But was he understanding the doctor's words correctly? Had Harmony broken confidentiality and shared his issues with this man?

This is not going well.

Jesse refrained from shaking his head. Sitting in his office chair, gazing into Pete's cool green eyes, he saw confidence and an iron will. This was not the Pete Harmony had described—weak and fragile. Nothing threw him. Not the mention of his sister or the video of a murder Jesse'd so carefully planned. This was a man who knew his own mind. A takedown was not going to be easy. Unless, of course, he could shake Pete's confidence in Harmony and plant doubts in his mind about her. As Jesse mulled over his next move, Pete suddenly made it easy for him.

"Did Dr. McKenna discuss my case with you?" Pete asked.

"She wanted my opinion about a few things."

"Isn't that unethical?"

"She told me she cleared it with you." Jesse wiped his upper lip.

Jesse saw the color fade from Pete's eyes. He'd wounded him. Betrayal was clearly a major trigger, and Pete must believe Harmony had betrayed him. This was perfect. Because of one off-handed remark he'd destroyed Pete's trust in Harmony. The next step would be to find a way to transfer that trust to Jesse.

Pete began to breathe in through his nose and exhale through his mouth. He did this several times before raising his arms and placing them behind his head. He continued to take deep breaths for a minute before he began to take shallow ones, puffing out the air in short bursts.

Jesse sat in silence, watching and waiting for what Pete would do next.

Pete put a hand on his chest and went back to deep breathing. Sweat appeared on his forehead. Tears leaked from his eyes. He was having a full-blown attack.

Pete suddenly stood up, and after turning back and forth like a robotic toy out of sync, he moved toward the door. Jesse sprang to his feet and took hold of Pete's upper arm. Pete remained docile and cooperative.

"Let's return to the chair and I'm going to help you." He guided Pete to a seated position. "Now I want you to listen to my voice. Let it calm you. Let it soothe you. When it tells you to breathe in, breathe in. When it says to breathe out, breathe out. Pete. Nod if you understand."

Pete nodded.

Jesse pulled his chair closer to Pete's and sat. "Look at me. Look in my eyes. Breathe in."

Pete breathed in.

"Breathe out."

Pete breathed out.

Jesse repeated this until Pete's oxygen intake stabilized.

"Now, Pete, it is very important that you relax. Let go and relax. I need you to stop trying to keep your emotions in check. You can turn them over to me. Let me take care of them for you. I can keep them in a safe place until you can handle them again. Just relax. Relax and let go. Now close your eyes."

Pete closed them.

"You are safe now, completely shielded from harm. I won't allow anything negative to come your way. As you listen to my voice, you have total confidence in what I am telling you. Complete trust. If you agree with that, nod."

Pete nodded.

Jesse couldn't believe his good fortune. With hypnosis he could establish Pete's subconscious reliance on him as a therapist and a friend and obliterate any remaining trust Pete might have in Harmony. Jesse was delighted.

He continued to talk Pete into a deep relaxed state. When he was convinced Pete was receptive, he told him he would only rely on him—Dr. Evans—for the truth, and whenever he heard the name Harmony he would feel repelled by her betrayal.

Pete suddenly spoke. "Darius says not to listen."

The statement threw Jesse for a loop. "Darius doesn't know what's best. Dr. Evans knows—"

"Darius says no."

Ire rose in Jesse's chest. Was it was possible that Pete had been hypnotized before by someone named Darius? "Who is Darius?"

Pete didn't respond.

"When I ask you a question, you are to answer. Do you understand?"

Pete nodded.

"Who is Darius?"

"Darius is many things."

Jesse frowned. "I don't understand. Is Darius a person?"

Pete nodded.

"Who is Darius to you?"

Pete shrugged.

"Who is Darius to you?" Jesse repeated with increased intensity.

"A spiritual helper."

Jesse was stumped. He'd never heard Harmony speak of a Darius in connection to Pete. He tried to think. He'd followed Pete around town a few times. Pete didn't actually go to many places. But then he remembered the time he went to North Hollywood and the strange man who had looked out the window.

"Does Darius live on Riverton?" Jesse asked.

Pete nodded.

Jesse grinned.

***

Harmony sat at a table in the Brew Company restaurant and checked her watch. It was ten after one. Jesse was late and she'd given him ten more minutes than she'd intended. She grabbed her purse and walked out.

Scurrying toward her car, she felt alternately empowered and weak. Empowered because she hadn't waited for Jesse, at least not for very long. Weak because she was forcing a change in her behavior which was proving to be somewhat tough.

She hopped in her vehicle and allowed herself to feel any and all emotions that came to the surface. Unfortunately, fear that she wouldn't sufficiently withstand Jesse's wrath at leaving the restaurant before he showed up grew the strongest. What could she do to reinforce her struggling independence from him? She decided to call a friend. She'd go dancing the way she used to. Jesse would hate that.

She took out her phone and viewed her contacts. Meagan was her first choice. They always had fun together. She punched in the number.

"Well, hello, stranger," Meagan said.

"I know. It's been a while."

"You call two years a while?"

"Has it been that long?" Harmony grimaced. She hadn't realized.

"Longer. I was trying to not twist the knife."

"Oops. Sorry."

"I know you are. I don't blame you. I blame Jesse. My God, was he rude the last time I saw him."

Harmony frowned. She never saw Jesse be anything but polite to Meagan. "He was? I didn't notice that."

"He always waited until you were out of the room."

Harmony hated this. She had been blind to so many things. "What did he say?"

"Something about how I was a bad influence because you were trying to do something important with your life and I was jealous, standing in your way."

"I never ever thought you were jealous or that you were standing in my way of anything. Why didn't you tell me?"

"I didn't think you'd believe me. You were so enamored."

"Well, I'm not anymore."

"You broke up? I figured that's why you called."

"Let's say I'm working on it. I'm in the process. Wanna help?"

"What did you have in mind?"

"The Manor House."

"Mmm. Swanky."

"Saturday night?" Harmony asked.

"Sunday."

"Sunday? Really?"

"I'm busy, but I don't want to turn you down. You might ghost me again."

Meagan's words were a stab to the heart. Why had she treated her friend so shabbily? "I didn't ghost you. Well, at least I didn't mean to. So, Sunday works. Pick you up?"

"I've moved."

"Well, give me your address and we'll call it a go."

"I'm still with Don. Mind if I bring him along? He'd love to see you."

"I'd love to see him."

"Should I find a fourth?"

Harmony took a deep breath. That was not a great idea. "Let's just leave it at us three."

"Understood."

After she got Meagan's information, they hung up. Harmony felt very pleased that they had reconnected and was excited for Sunday to come around. She reached to start the car but stopped when she saw Jesse's Mercedes enter the parking lot. If he saw her, he'd confront her. She could hear it now. *My God, Harmony, I was only fifteen minutes late!*

When he was in a position where she thought he couldn't see, she started the car and zoomed away. Now she had to be prepared for the inevitable phone call. He'd always had a stronger will than she did, and she tended to acquiesce. But she was resolute this time. She would not allow anything he said to deter her. Complete independence was the mission. She'd intended to break up in person, but since he'd disrespected her once again by being late, she gave herself permission to do it over the phone.

As she drove her stomach churned. When had she become such a pushover?

Spineless and stupid.

Let's not take it that far, she told herself. After all, she was taking steps and they weren't exactly baby steps.

But that need for a sounding board, for someone to help keep her strong, reared its head. Once again, the name Darius popped into her brain.

Oh, what the hell. Why not?

She drove to North Hollywood.

Chapter 20

Darius opened the door and Harmony marched right in.

"Welcome," Darius said, amusement in his tone.

"Sorry," Harmony responded. "I know I'm being presumptuous." She led the way to his office or counseling room—whatever he called it—and opened the door. "I need to talk to someone."

"And you have no one else?"

She noticed that she was standing beside the donation basket. She opened her purse, took a fifty from her wallet and dropped it in.

"That isn't necessary," Darius said.

"No, I'm here for your help. I'm not a mooch." She sat on the love seat where she'd been before. "Is this all right?"

"Wherever makes you comfortable."

"I figure Andrea wanted me to seek you out so she must know something I don't about you."

Darius smiled and placed his fingertips together. "*That* may be true. But don't think because someone has died they have all the answers. Most are just as clueless as when they were on Earth."

"See. You say things like that and . . . and . . . I don't know. It sounds so high and mighty. What makes you the expert?"

He closed his eyes and tilted his head.

"I'm sorry. I don't know why I'm so rude to you," Harmony said.

"No need to be sorry. It is a reflection of you, not me."

Harmony's fingers went to her head and she growled. "See? There you go again! High and mighty!"

He said nothing.

"Let's start over," Harmony said.

"Let's get centered," Darius said. "I don't think you know why you're here and I don't know why either. Maybe I have a message for you that I am unaware of. Shall we see?"

"By all means." She motioned to go ahead with one hand. Why couldn't she be this forthright and strong with Jesse?

Darius sat on the floor, crossed his legs, back straight, and closed his eyes. Harmony stared at him. He remained in this seated position without so much as a twitch for twenty minutes before he opened his eyes.

"Andrea is not coming through. All I'm getting is a bit of what I got before. Beware of the man with the tan VW. Also, a feeling that you'd be better off not going out Sunday night."

"How do you know what I'm doing Sunday night?"

"I don't. I'm merely conveying a feeling I received."

"Well, I better go." She rose to her feet.

Darius stood up. "By all means. Just watch out for your friend."

"My friend?"

"I didn't receive a name."

Harmony took a deep breath and closed her eyes. Did he somehow know she'd reconnected with Meagan? That was impossible. He'd merely thrown out a statement to see if she'd bite. He was a huckster. Why had she been so silly as to seek him out?

"I came here to feel better, not to worry," Harmony said, opening her eyes.

"Don't worry. Watch out for your friend." He put his prayerful hands together.

What Harmony really wanted to talk about was Jesse. But what could this man have to say about that? Give her the male perspective? No. She didn't get the impression he'd take sides. She really had cut everyone out of her life if she was running to someone like Darius to talk to. He was a hack!

For a brief moment she thought about contacting her estranged mother to see if anything had changed and decided against it. Her mother had made it clear long ago, she'd had Harmony when she was too young. She'd raised her. She'd done her job. Harmony had only ever been a stumbling block to her happiness. Harmony had made peace with the situation long ago. It would accomplish nothing to go drilling in that well. Anyway, she felt better. She felt calmer. "Thank you," she said as she walked out the door.

"*Namaste.*"

***

When Jesse saw that Harmony had not waited for him in the restaurant, he turned around and left. Immediately he called her number, but she didn't answer. It was just as well. He would have picked a fight. His plans for Harmony were changing from moment to moment. She was becoming way too independent. He might do away with her, too. He just might.

Jesse jumped into his Mercedes and decided he should check out who this Darius was that seemed to be interfering with his plan for Pete. Traffic was cooperative and soon he was parking across the street from the apartment building just as he'd done before. He unbuckled his seat belt and grabbed hold of the door handle when he froze. What the hell was Harmony doing coming out of Darius' place? She traveled down the steps and was at her car before Jesse had a clue what to do. Accost her on the street? That seemed unwise.

Instead of making a move, he watched her drive away. He would, however, talk to Darius. He stepped out of the car and jogged across the street. He took the stairs two at a time and forcefully rapped on Darius' door. No one answered. He knew Darius had to be home because Harmony had just been inside. He rapped even harder. This time he heard a voice from the courtyard.

"May I help you?"

Jesse turned and looked over the railing. A heavyset woman in her fifties with short blond hair and large eighties-style glasses stared up at him. When he smiled, she smiled back.

"Are you looking for an apartment? That one's for rent," the woman said.

"It is?" Confused, Jesse glanced at the large window, but the blinds were closed and he couldn't see inside. "I thought someone named Darius lived here."

"Not there. That apartment's been empty for nearly a year. People walk in and walk right back out."

"I'm looking for Darius."

She shook her head. "No Darius."

"And no one lives here?"

"Everyone who takes a look thinks the place is spooky. Go figure. I've had the place painted. I leave the curtains open to let in the sun when anyone takes a look. I did have a young woman give me a deposit for about five seconds. She gave me the money. Went back up to take another look and asked for her deposit back. Said she heard some weird noise she didn't like and it felt creepy. Like someone was already living there. It's very strange."

"Yes," agreed Jesse. "That is."

The blonde began moseying back to her unit. Jesse bounded down the stairs. Was Harmony looking for a new place to live? No. The manager would have said. Well, he'd just ask Harmony what she was doing there when they talked. And she'd better have an answer he could swallow.

***

Finally Guerrero had something to go on. The GPS data for Mrs. Lyman's phone indicated that Jordan had driven to Lucerne Valley. Mrs. Lyman informed him that Jordan didn't know anyone in Lucerne Valley, at least no one he'd ever mentioned. Because the phone was an android and had no tracking software installed, the diligent cop had to rely on cell phone tower pings to coordinate the location. He enlisted the most qualified expert in the department to help him, and he'd come up with a large desert area in Lucerne Valley that needed to be searched. Guerrero made a call to the San Bernardino County Sheriff's department for their assistance. He told them that he was trying to locate a car last driven by a possible murder victim named Jordan Lyman, connected to the Archibald Bent case. Had they heard of that?

Three hours later Guerrero received a call that they'd located the car. It had been abandoned in the middle of nowhere, empty—no body in the trunk and no sign that anyone had been killed in the car.

"You need to process the scene as if you did find a body," he told the sheriff's deputy. "Take impressions of nearby tire tracks, footprints. Dust for prints. The works. You need to bring in a detective and have him call me. If my guy was murdered, it would have happened on your patch."

Chapter 21

After ducking Jesse's calls, deleting his messages, and not answering the door the one time he'd come knocking, Harmony decided she was tired of walking on eggshells. Dressed to the nines in her new jumpsuit, ready to have a good time with her friends, she finally answered the phone.

"You were late again," she said omitting the hello. "I'm done."

"I was with Pete. That's why I was late."

That piece of news caused Harmony to deflate like a helium balloon shot with an arrow. She sank to the bed and sat. "What? How did that happen?"

"He called. Remember you told him about me? Wanting to consult?"

Harmony had to clear her throat before she could talk. "I remember."

"He had a full blown anxiety attack and I had to talk him down. It took some time. I couldn't leave him. I'm sorry I was late. I didn't mean to be."

Jesse's voice had that buttery quality he used when he wanted to sweet-talk someone. She'd heard it before. Harmony pictured a purring cat lying on its back, looking for a tummy rub. "I'm glad you were there for him," she said, straightening her back, steeling her will.

She heard Jesse sigh. "I'm doing this for you."

"Well, that's not good. You should be doing it for him."

"Well, of course. But I know how much he means to you and if I can help him, I'm helping you. Can I come over?"

There it was. The dreaded question. She wondered if he was already at the house, on her doorstep or in his car. Leaving the light on in the bedroom, she rushed to the living room, left it dark and peered out the window. She didn't see his Dodge or his Mercedes and felt reassured.

"Uh. I'm going out with friends," she informed him.

"Oh? Who?"

She didn't answer right away.

"Harmony, it's obvious you're on edge and as much as I hate it, I see the writing on the wall. But it's been six years. There is absolutely no reason we can't trust each other and still care about each other. You have to know I will always love you."

Her heart began to pound. "I know. I'm sorry."

"So? Who are you meeting?"

"Remember Meagan?"

"Yes, I think I do."

"Her and Ron."

"No one else?"

"No. No one else." The question irked her but she tried not to allow it to show in her voice.

"Okay, well. I better let you go," he said. "Oh, one more thing. Pete mentioned someone named Darius. Do you know him?"

"I've met him."

"Do you know where he lives?"

"Why?"

"Harmony, please. Why are you so defensive?"

"In Noho on Riverton." Jesse was silent. "Hello?"

"I'm here. Like I said. I better let you go. Have a good time. I mean that." He hung up.

Harmony hoped he meant it. She went into the master bathroom and examined her makeup. She was going to have a good time tonight. She poked dangly earrings through her ears and put Jesse out of her mind.

***

Two hours later, Jesse was following Harmony to the Manor House in his truck. She didn't know the Chevy Colorado so even if she spotted it, she'd have no reason to think he was behind the wheel. He parked on the street where he could see the parking lot, left the motor running, and watched. She went into the club alone. She'd meet her friends inside. He pulled out the knife he'd brought from under the seat. If the opportunity arose, why not? He never did like Meagan. Always making snide remarks, sowing seeds of distrust. What a bitch.

He drove on and parked a block away. He walked back, the knife safely stashed from view in a sheath beneath his jacket. A ball cap positioned low on his head hid his face. The building would have cameras and he didn't want to be recognized. He stood away from the building and rested against a Toyota Highlander. It might be a long night for nothing. But then again, one never knew.

***

The Manor House was packed, even on a Sunday night. The live band was great. Spotlights glared, the disco balls shone, the saxophone ranged from honky and aggressive to smooth and sweet. Harmony boogied up a storm and didn't even mind when the strangers she danced with suddenly noticed her scar and reacted. Alcohol erased people's filters. Their jaws dropped. They asked questions. Harmony made up a story.

"I was a cesarean baby. The doctor cut too deep."

"Are you shittin' me?"

"Why would I do that? Would you like to touch?"

Some did. Some didn't. Some didn't want to dance with her anymore, as if scars were catching. She found it amusing.

"Ahhh," she bellowed, joining Meagan and Don at their table, collapsing onto the seat. "This is fantastic. I haven't gone dancing in years." She picked up her club soda and sipped. They'd been there nearly three hours and Harmony had limited herself to two glasses of wine.

Meagan was tipsy and was digging through her purse. "I can't find it," she complained.

"She left her phone in the car," Don said.

"No, I didn't."

Don motioned at his girlfriend with his thumb and shook his head. "She won't believe me. She's worried."

"Why would I leave it in the car?" Meagan asked, annoyed.

"By accident," he said.

"Oh, yeah."

Harmony chuckled. "What do you need it for?"

"I want to order pizza."

"Now?" Don asked.

"No." Meagan eyed her surroundings. "For later."

"Then order it later, after we leave," Don said.

"I'm going to get it." She stood up, off balance. "Whoa." Don tried to pull her back, but she rebuffed him by grabbing his wrist and shoving it aside. "I'm just going to the car."

"Oh, don't do that," Harmony said.

"I want my phone!" She marched off through the sea of people.

Instantly Harmony thought of Darius' warning.

Watch out for your friend.

"Go with her," Harmony told Don.

"No. I hate it when she gets like this."

Harmony stood up and tried to edge past Don.

"She'll be fine," he insisted.

"Well, I want to make sure."

"Then I'll go," Don said. He turned but standing up was difficult. He was blocked by a crowd of young people standing very close. He accidentally jostled a pretty brunette who resembled Ariana Grande and her drink spilled on him.

"Watch it," she said.

"I'll watch you," he responded. "Let me buy you another?"

She smiled, apparently not put off by the obvious and stale come-on. "Okay," she cooed.

Harmony watched Don crane his neck for the bar. If someone was going to look after Meagan it would have to be her. She also knew if they all left the table, they'd lose it. She pulled Don back to his seat. "Wait for the drink girl. I'm going after Meagan."

Don shrugged and turned his attention to "Ariana." "Guess we'll have to wait."

Harmony took off for the door, fighting her way through the crowd. She didn't even know where Meagan and Don had parked. She'd have to walk around and search.

Jesse spotted tipsy Meagan immediately. He kept his body low as he jogged across the street to the Manor House parking lot. He maintained several yards' distance from his prey, doing his best to stay in the shadows and avoid people who were milling around in the lot. His movements captured the occasional observer's attention, but for the most part the club goers were only interested in their own good time and personal circle of friends.

He moved between the cars, watching Meagan stumble toward her vehicle. "Pizza!" she called out. "Piiizzzaaa!"

Shut up, Jesse thought. *You'll have people looking*.

He glanced over his shoulder and saw one person look in Meagan's direction. He stopped until the lookie-loo returned her attention to her clique. Jesse set his sights on Meagan again and crept closer. Her car was parked away from the building, amid an ocean of cars in an area that wasn't well lit.

I'll have enough cover, Jesse thought. *I just have to be quick.*

Meagan's car chirped as the passenger door unlocked. She opened it and leaned in.

Jesse made a game plan in his head. He would grab the bitch and hold her with one hand slapped over her mouth. He was big and muscular, while she was slight and probably weighed all of one hundred and ten pounds. There shouldn't be a problem. It would be a pleasure to cut her and drop her in her tracks. And who knew? Maybe Harmony would come looking for her friend and find her personally. He wished he could hang around to see that, but he wouldn't be able to. Once he plunged the knife he would have to be off. He took his weapon from its sheath and inched closer.

Meagan came out of the car, phone in hand. "*Voila!*" She teetered like a pendulum, slammed the door closed, and spun round. Jesse was about to swoop in when he heard footsteps and Harmony's voice.

"There you are. Thank you, sir."

Jesse quickly ducked behind a Honda.

"Not a problem," a male voice said.

Jesse peered around the side of the car and saw a security guard standing nearby as Harmony took hold of her friend. "You know what? I think we should go find Don and get the hell out of here. Then we can all go to Pizza Guys. What do you think?"

"Do you know I like anchovies?" Meagan asked.

"I did not know that."

Meagan laughed. "I'm lying." She threw her arms over Harmony.

Harmony led her back toward the dance club, security strolling alongside.

Jesse had missed his chance. He stood up, forgetting he still held the knife in his hand. It glinted under a parking lot light as he turned to go, shocking a female patron coming for her car. She backed away with a scream so shrill Jesse feared his eardrums would burst. There was no time to kill her and get away. He could already hear others coming. As she ran toward people, Jesse sprinted across the busy street, dodging cars like a basketball player zigzagging past the opposing team. Once safely on the other side, he ducked behind a car parked at the curb and caught his breath. After a minute he poked his head up. He could see activity in the parking lot, but no one was headed his way. In the confusion he'd made a clean escape. He ducked back down and waited another couple of minutes before he began to calmly walk to his truck. He didn't want to draw unwanted attention by appearing to be trying to "get away." Not with the knife . . . he felt for it and realized he'd dropped it.

"Don't panic," he told himself. *No one was stabbed. It's a good knife. If someone finds it they'll probably keep it. If security gets hold of it . . .*

The entire drive home Jesse had a frank conversation with himself. He'd been reckless of late. Partnering up to commit murder had been a major misstep. Hopefully killing Jordan and dumping his car had rectified it. Hawkeye was unfortunate, but what was he supposed to do? And why had it become so important to him to take out Meagan just to hurt Harmony?

He still intended to kill Pete. And Harmony had to go. He'd made up his mind about that. But he needed to smarten up. Once those two were history, he'd take a break. Then, after a while he'd return to the person he was pre-Harmony, pre-Mr.-Upstanding-Citizen, pre-I-intend-to- follow-the-law. He'd go back to making his own rules. No one would be the wiser.

Chapter 22

Detective Guerrero could see that Detective Hernandez was pleased with the information she'd discovered about Dr. Jesse Evans, as was he. The data spread out on his desk didn't prove he was their killer; the man had a pristine record. But there was one big red flag. Dr. Evans owned property in Lucerne Valley.

"There could be a perfectly innocent explanation for Jordan's car being in the vicinity of Dr. Evans' property," he told Hernandez. "Jordan could have been feeling the heat put on by yours truly and gone to see his old therapist to help him cope."

"And while he was out there he could've met with foul play from someone other than Dr. Evans. You don't believe that though, do you, sir?"

"No. I don't. Call it Guerrero's gut." He patted his tummy.

"Neither do I. Call it Hernandez' hunch." She tapped her temple. They both chuckled.

"We're going to have to come up with more," Guerrero said.

"Well, he does own four vehicles."

"Tire tracks by Jordan's car. Very good. Does he own a truck?"

"Sure does. A big ol' Chevy Colorado."

"That would tow a car in the desert without a problem."

"It sure would."

Guerrero stopped leaning back in his chair and it squawked with the shifting of his weight. "You know, this is when most detectives would say it's time to pay Dr. Evans a call. My gut says no. I like the idea that he's in the dark. He has no idea we're looking into him. If I did talk to him what do you think he'd say?"

Hernandez answered, "Why, of course my number's on Jordan's phone. He called to make appointments. As for his car being in the desert . . ." She paused to give it some thought.

"He'd either say Jordan never showed or he'd admit that he saw him and he left. I don't have any leverage to make him fess up. However, he might think it strange that we haven't contacted him to ask about Jordan since he was a client."

"You should at least give him a call."

"That's what I'm thinking. But I won't tell him we found Jordan's car. Who knows? If I rattle his cage just a little he might let something slip."

"Right."

"In the meantime, we need to know what tires are on that Chevy Colorado. And Thacker and Haynes need something to do."

Hernandez laughed. "Want me to hit them up?"

"If you'd be so kind."

She pushed out of the chair, eager to be of service.

Guerrero reached for his desk phone. First he would call Detective Horton, the contact he'd been given with the San Bernardino sheriff's office. Then he'd call Jesse Evans.

"I was about to give you a ring," Horton said. "Got some news. The car was clean. Nothing to indicate someone was killed in it. And it was wiped down. No prints."

"I suppose it was too much to hope for to find Evans' prints."

"We found Lyman's phone, just like we thought we would, and we found something else."

"I'm all ears."

"There was a burner in the trunk."

"Nice."

"Don't ask me why he didn't pitch it, but he didn't. We checked the call log. It was used to phone Evans twelve times. Once *after* the murder of Archibald Bent."

"Now that's something." Guerrero smiled. They were getting somewhere.

"I think so," Horton agreed.

"And guess what?" Guerrero said. "Evans owns property in Lucerne."

"No kidding."

"He could be holding Jordan there. Think that would get us a warrant to snoop around?"

"Hmmm. A bit thin, but maybe. You really think he's kidnapped him?"

"I think he's killed him," Guerrero said bluntly.

Horton was quiet.

"Look. You took pictures and casts of the tire tracks, right?" Guerrero asked.

"Right."

"I'm working on getting prints of Evans' truck tracks. If they match up . . ." Guerrero shrugged.

"We've got our warrant," Horton finished.

"Honestly, though, I don't even know if he has the truck here in L.A. or if he keeps it in Lucerne Valley. Could you cozy up to the neighbors? Find out what they know."

"I was just going to suggest that," Horton said.

"Great minds," responded Guerrero.

***

Jesse didn't like what he saw on the morning news. "Fright in Manor House Parking Lot," the caption read. It was a small story—an interview with a girl who saw a man with a knife. "No, he never tried to hurt me, just scared me silly," she said. "But I could see he wanted to."

"They always embellish," Jesse said, grabbing a favorite tie from the closet tie rack.

The kicker to the story was the video footage. Cameras had caught glimpses of what the police termed as a highly suspicious male moving about the lot. The face was unrecognizable because of distance, video quality, and his ball cap. Also, in most shots, his back was to the camera. The police wanted to talk to this male and urged him to come in for an interview.

"Fat chance," Jesse mumbled, tossing the tie around his neck and tucking it under the collar of his dress shirt.

Okay, he didn't need to worry about the missing knife. Didn't sound like they had it. But he was done pussyfooting around. Pete was coming in. If he couldn't hypnotize him and get him to come willingly to Lucerne, he was going to bite the bullet and drug him.

He tied the tie with ease and made certain he had the dimple and knot displayed perfectly. He was reaching for a tie bar when his cell rang. He grabbed it. The ID told him it was the City of Los Angeles Police.

It crossed his mind not to answer. But that would merely delay the inevitable. Someone must have turned in his knife after all. But he didn't think the police would have processed it this quickly. They could have, he supposed. How long did it take to find prints on a knife? And his prints would be on file because of some volunteer work he did with Social Services a few years back. The knife might have been a priority since the parking lot incident made the news. He took a deep breath.

"Hello."

"Dr. Evans?"

"Yes."

"I'm Detective Guerrero with the Los Angeles Police. I was hoping for a moment of your time."

"Is this about my knife?" Jesse grimaced. He was thinking the question and didn't mean to verbalize it.

"No. What about a knife?"

"Oh, nothing. I lost a hunting knife. It's no big deal. Really. How can I help you?" How stupid could he be? No stupider than the police. He told himself not to worry.

"I was wondering if you've heard from Jordan Lyman. I understand he's a client of yours."

"*Was* a client of mine. He isn't currently. I haven't spoken to him in a while. Why?"

"He's missing."

"Missing?"

"Yes. We've been talking to him because of his connection to Archibald Bent. Did you hear about that?"

"It was all over the news, so yes."

"We think Jordan couldn't take the pressure and did a runner."

Jesse smiled. They thought Jordan ran away. "I suppose that's a logical assumption."

"Is it? Is he the sort of person who runs from his problems?"

"I can't really discuss him with you, now can I, detective?"

"Is there anything you can tell me about him? Something that might reveal where he'd go?"

"Not really. I mean . . ." Jesse paused. It might be better to say nothing. Then again, if he could influence the detective to move away from any interest in Jordan it was worth a shot. "Let me just say this. I wouldn't put my focus on Jordan. I always thought he was a good kid. I can't see him doing anything really bad."

"Oh, doctor. We both know how surprising human beings can be. Did *you* know Archibald Bent?"

What sort of mind fuck question is that? Jesse he took a breath and held his temper. "No. I never met the man. Didn't know him at all."

"I didn't think so."

"Well, detective. I need to be off if I'm going to meet with my client on time."

"Of course. Thank you for your time."

Guerrero hung up first, leaving Jesse to listen to his quick-beating heart. They'd connected him to Jordan. He knew they would because he'd been his therapist. But if that was all they had, he told himself, he was in the clear.

***

Guerrero thought about Dr. Evans' odd question, *Is this about my knife?*

What knife? Had something happened with a knife that would escalate to the attention of the department? He called to a deputy standing at a nearby desk. "Hey, Acosta. Is there some incident with a knife I don't know about? Something that just happened. I know the question's kind of vague . . ." Guerrero tossed up his hands.

"A female claimed she was nearly attacked with one at the Manor House last night. Made the news, but she wasn't hurt. And in talking to her, from what she said, it's pretty iffy that he meant her harm."

"Did the guy lose his knife?"

"Not that I know of. It's kind of a non-story really, except I guess you don't want some nut running around town with a knife threatening people, if that's what he was doing."

"Thanks." Guerrero put his coat on. Maybe he'd have a look-see around the Manor House parking lot. The worst that could happen is he'd come up empty.

***

Plain clothes detective Bob Horton was an attractive man in his mid-thirties who loved his job and preferred rural life to the big city. He tended to trust the judgment of his fellow detectives, especially those with a lifetime of experience, like Donato Guerrero. He felt honored to be working with him. Technically, it was the other way around. Guerrero was working with Horton, since Jordan Lyman's vehicle had been found in Horton's jurisdiction. Right now the young man was considered a missing person, not a murder victim, but he was also a person of interest in the Archibald Bent case, and the sophomore detective was happy to be helping with that.

Before he walked out of the station to his Jeep Grand Cherokee, Horton had sussed out who Evans' neighbors were. A man named Albert Perkins lived the closest. He gave Mr. Perkins a call and quickly received an earful. "Call me Al" was only too happy to meet Horton at the gate to Jesse Evans' drive and tell him everything he knew.

When Horton pulled up, Al was waiting for him in a blue Dodge pickup. "Let's go in," Al shouted through the open window of the cab, pointing at the gate.

"Uhh . . ." Horton responded.

"Hey, my friend lives here and he gave me carte blanche. I got the code."

"Okay then. I guess it's not a problem."

"Nope. Above board and all that." Al swung his truck into position and punched in the correct digits. Horton followed Al along the gravel drive to the garage.

Al hopped down from the cab and Horton climbed out of the Jeep. "Like I said on the phone, I reported Hawkeye missing, but you cops said he had the right to disappear. So that was that. But I'm telling you, it's all fishy. If he was leaving, he would have said goodbye. And that Evans is as slippery as a greased pig."

Al opened the garage door.

"I found that propane tank right where Hawkeye said it was. I took it, too. No charging me with theft now. I just borrowed it. But anyways, while that's interesting, here's the more interesting part."

He walked to Jesse's VW bug parked in the leftmost space.

"A Volkswagen bug." Horton nodded and rubbed his temple. "Katie Hammel that went missing in Big Bear. That's what you're thinking."

"Yep. And you should be, too. First this Jordan you're interested in. Then Hawkeye. And Katie makes three. Three strikes you're out. It's a good saying and a sure bet."

"Well, it's just a car and a theory. We need proof."

"Take the bug."

"Can't do that."

"Didn't think so. But let me show you something else."

He walked away from the garage and the house, traveling a distance of several yards. Horton trailed.

"Yeah, I'm snoopy," Al said. "I nosed around. I don't care what people call me. But here." He stopped walking and pointed straight down. "That's blood."

Horton knew he couldn't be sure without testing, but it was a possibility. A rusty-colored substance had certainly stained the ground in spotty shapes.

"I think it's Hawkeye's. So I took some." He slipped a plastic sandwich bag from his back pocket and held it out to Horton.

Reluctantly the detective took it. It felt like he was breaking all the rules, although he didn't think he was. This guy was a private citizen who'd been invited onto the property by his friend who lived there.

"It is in plain sight," Horton said. "But, ah . . ."

"You need to gather the sample yourself." Al handed him an unused sandwich bag.

Horton smiled. "And, I need something of Hawkeye's to compare it to."

"Not a problem. I got a key to his living quarters. Let's go find something."

***

Pete lay on the proverbial couch in Dr. Evans' office. He was relaxed and calm and self aware. What he wasn't, was hypnotized. Despite the doctor's best efforts, he kept remembering Darius' words from his previous time in the office, and it kept the doctor's suggestions from penetrating. However, he played along. He wanted to know what therapy Dr. Evans was going for.

"I believe you need to get out of the city," Jesse said. "Not a lot of people know this, but I own a ranch. Sixty acres where the air is clean and the surrounding mountains are beautiful. Sounds nice, doesn't it?"

"Yes," Pete said.

"Would you like to see it?"

"Yes."

"Good. Because we're going there. You and me, together. So, come on. Get on your feet."

Pete stood and waited for further instruction.

"Give me your phone."

Pete did as instructed. Jesse gave Pete the keys to his Dodge.

"Now I want you to take the elevator to the lower level parking. Do you understand?"

Pete nodded.

"My car is in space 21. Sit in the passenger seat and wait for me. Can you do that?"

"Yes," said Pete.

"Okay. Go."

Pete walked out. Jesse turned off Pete's phone and waited five minutes before he followed.

***

The manager of the Manor House nightclub sat with Guerrero at a computer in the security office and pointed at the screen. "This one caught the best view. It happens here, in this lower left corner of the monitor."

Guerrero saw a man turn his back to the camera just as a young woman approached, grew terrified, and screamed. There was no way in hell to tell if the man was Jesse Evans from this angle. If Guerrero happened to get lucky and find the knife, and it had Evans' prints on it, that would be a different story. He watched the man slink away and made note of the general direction he took. That would tell Guerrero where to look.

"Is there another camera angle? And can you back it up so I can see what happened before the incident?" Guerrero asked.

The manager complied.

Guerrero watched Meagan looking for her cell phone. A man was crouched behind a car watching her, but again, his back was to the camera and he was only partially seen. The man pulled back out of view when Harmony and a security guard approached Meagan.

"That woman looks familiar to me," Guerrero said.

"Yeah?" responded the manager. "She's kind of far away."

"It's the way she walks. Do you have video of the door? I'd like to see her face."

"That would be camera one," the manager said, typing on the keyboard. "And we're talking just a couple minutes earlier." He manipulated the video to the appropriate time.

Guerrero watched. When he saw what he wanted, he nearly leapt out of the chair. "Freeze it."

The manager hit pause. Guerrero gasped. That was the woman with the scar on her face he'd seen with Wayne Hoffman. He stared at the video. He didn't know her name, but Wayne would.

"I need copies of these videos. And any others that could have caught images of this woman and the man with the knife."

"Not a problem."

By the time Detective Guerrero returned to the station he'd talked to Wayne Hoffman. The woman in the video was Dr. Harmony McKenna, Pete Ashton's ex-therapist. Guerrero also had the lost knife in his possession which he promptly dropped off at the lab. He'd found it in the gutter. Luckily no one had picked it up. Now, if the knife revealed Jesse Evans' prints, he had something.

Guerrero thought things through. Archibald Bent had a vendetta against Andrea Ashton. Andrea was Pete's sister. Pete had been Harmony McKenna's client. Jesse was a therapist. If Jesse knew Harmony, he had his connection to Archibald. A thin one, but a connection just the same.

Guerrero let loose with a long, low whistle that took the place of the happy dance he used to do when he was thirty pounds lighter and twenty years younger.

Chapter 23

Jesse licked his lips as if he'd just devoured the most delectable dessert. Pete sat in the kitchen of his Lucerne Valley house, tied to one of the dining room chairs. Zip ties bound his ankles to the chair legs. A belt cinched him to the chair back. His hands were secured behind him with a length of rope. His chin drooped downward and would have rested on his chest if he weren't restrained. Jesse had drugged him once they got to the house. Pete had started grumbling about the long ride and Jesse immediately knew he wasn't hypnotized. He soothed away Pete's apprehension as best he could and once they arrived at their destination, Jesse suggested a cold drink. He gave him a soda laced with Ambien.

"All right!" Jesse cheered, clapping his hands together once. "Let's get this party started." He took out his cell and called Harmony. Naturally she didn't pick up. She'd been avoiding him. But that didn't matter. Once she listened to the message he was going to leave, she would not only call. She'd drop everything and be at Scarlett in a hot minute.

"Harmony, it's me. I'm with Pete. There's been an accident and well, just call me. I'll explain." He turned his face away. "Pete. Pete. Don't try to move. Just lie still. I called Harmony. I'm sure she'll be here as soon as she can."

He hung up and laughed. If that didn't make her come running, nothing would. He was so excited his emotions zoomed up and down like an out-of whack escalator.

Hurry up, Harmony. Call me back.

He began to pace.

Now how are you going to kill them?

He stopped pacing and took a second to glare at his phone.

Harmony, call!

He began to pace again.

Pete's to die first. Yes, that's right. Harmony gets to watch.

He tossed his head back and let loose with a low guttural growl.

Where is that bitch!

She'll call. She'll call. Don't worry. She'll call.

She better!

He stopped pacing.

What's that smell?

Jesse whipped around and faced the stove. He smelled gas! Had he accidently turned on a burner that didn't ignite? The odor was faint, but detectible. He examined the stove top. Everything was off. He opened the oven door. No gas smell came from there. Shit! He didn't need this. He couldn't call the gas company to come out. What would he do with Pete?

Suddenly the odor was gone.

He chalked it up to a hallucination. He was overly excited and worried that something would go wrong at the same time.

Dammit! Where is that bitch?

Ten minutes passed before the phone finally rang.

"Harmony?"

"What happened? Is Peter all right?"

"Not really. He fell off a horse." He wiped his upper lip.

"What? What was he doing on a horse?"

"I can take a lot of time to explain it now or you can jump in your car and get out here as fast as you can."

"Where are you?"

"I have a ranch in Lucerne Valley."

"You what? When did that happen?"

Jesse threw his free hand up in the air in frustration and thought, *What's wrong with you? I thought you loved Pete and here you are wasting time with stupid questions.*

"A while ago," he responded, trying to sound composed. If he pressed too hard she might sense something was off and not come. He decided to try a different tack. "Look. If you don't want to drive out here, I understand. It's just he was asking for you and I know how much you care, so . . ."

"No, I'm coming. Of course I'm coming. I was just surprised. Did you call the paramedics?"

He wanted to scream.

"When you get here," he said, "drive around back and park in the garage. I haven't repaired the opener yet, so I'll leave the door up for you. Here's the address and code to the gate. Do you have a pen?"

After he hung up, he had to calm himself. He needed a task. He would put the Dodge away. With no Hawkeye to help, he'd left it outside.

"Now you don't go anywhere, Pete, ya hear?" Jesse said with a wink.

Pete didn't move.

"That's a good boy."

Jesse walked to the garage and was about to slide the right door up when he spotted something that concerned him. It wasn't down all the way. There was a good three-inch gap between the bottom of the door and the concrete. He didn't believe he'd left it that way.

Then again, maybe he had. The garage didn't have a lock. Closing it all the way wouldn't have stopped a vandal. God, he hoped that wasn't going to start up again. He needed a new Hawkeye.

Dismissing the garage as unimportant he raised the door. Sunlight flooded the floor and he stopped cold. He saw footsteps that didn't belong to him. Someone had been here. He checked the VW. It looked fine. There really wasn't anything worth taking except the car. He didn't own a lot of tools.

The propane tank!

He whirled around. It was gone. That nosy guy with the big mouth had come onto his property and stolen it. The asshole. *Asshole!* Did he think Jesse wouldn't notice? He could care less about the propane, but he hated the disrespect. He might have to do something about that. He just might.

But not now.

Jesse made a noise of disgust and hopped into the Dodge. As he parked the car he thought, *Right now I've got bigger fish to fry.*

***

"Are you sitting down?" Horton asked Guerrero over the phone.

"As a matter of fact I'm walking back from the toilet. I'm on my sixth cup of coffee. What's up?" Guerrero dropped into his chair, cell to his ear, chair squawk beneath his butt.

"I got enough for a warrant."

"Really? Because I can be out of here in a split second. I want to be there."

"Already took a look around. The warrant wasn't for the house. Just the garage and the grounds. Evans wasn't home."

Guerrero reached for his coffee mug, thought better of it, and pushed it away. "So what did you find?"

"The neighbor, Al Perkins, took pictures with his phone of the truck's tire tracks in the garage. They left something to be desired, but they still provided enough detail to be a fair match to the tracks left near Jordan's car. Since the neighbor took the photos, the judge was okay with it."

"I'm glad about the tires because Thacker and Haynes came up empty. Said they couldn't locate the vehicle. But we'll be able to get clear impressions from the actual tires once we find the truck."

"Right. Also, I took a dirt sample that looked suspicious. We tested it and found it was contaminated with human blood. We don't know whose. That will come later. Anyway, we went back in there and took official photographs. Took more samples of the dirt with the blood. It gets windy out here so we didn't find footprints leading up to or away from the bloody ground. That was disappointing."

"Yeah," Guerrero sighed.

"There's a couple more things that need to be investigated in regards to Evans. He had a hired hand, a caretaker named Hawkeye, who's gone missing according to the neighbor. This neighbor, this Al, thinks that blood in the dirt is going to match up to him. Al had a key to the place where Hawkeye lived and we looked around for something that would have some of his DNA. We came up empty. It appears he packed up and left."

"That's interesting."

"There's more. This is very circumstantial and wouldn't mean a thing without all the other facts. But a girl went missing in Big Bear and she was last seen getting into a VW bug. Evans has a bug in his garage."

Guerrero nodded and grinned. His gut was liking this information more and more. "I think it's time to bring this guy in for a proper chat."

Guerrero called Jesse's cell and it went to voice mail. He left a message asking Jesse to come to the station to answer some questions. Guerrero's gut began to gurgle and even a ginger chew didn't settle it down. He sent officers to Jesse's office and to his home in Sherman Oaks. Jesse was nowhere to be found.

He decided Jesse must have gone to Lucerne Valley. He called Detective Horton. "Are you going to apply for a warrant to check out the VW and to get inside the house?"

"I'm ten steps ahead of you. I already did. I think I'll get it, too. The neighbor may think that blood is Hawkeye's, but I'll wager it's Jordan Lyman's. I mean, he's missing, and we found his car with those tire tracks that most likely belong to Evans."

"Something's going on for Evans to not pick up his phone. I'm driving out there. I'll see you in what? Two and a half hours?"

"Depending on traffic."

"Yeah." Guerrero hung up and his gut settled down. It did that sometimes when it was in agreement with what the experienced cop decided to do.

Chapter 24

Harmony arrived at Scarlett in her blue Kia. It had taken over three hours to reach Lucerne Valley because traffic had been thick and slow. Luckily there were no accidents, just too many cars and semis. She put in the gate code and drove to the garage. As she rolled closer she saw something she didn't expect.

"Is that a Volkswagen bug?" she whispered in awe.

She parked the car and walked over to have a look. It was a tan, late 1960's style VW. Nerves prickled her throat and she began to breathe a little quicker. Darius had mentioned a VW. Not only that, the entire drive to the High Desert, he'd tried to get in her head and she'd blocked him. Now she wished she hadn't. Had he been trying to warn her? If so, about what? Or who? Jesse? With her back to the house she stared at the VW, adrift in a sense of dread. The crunch of footsteps approached behind her and intense fear sprinted up her spine.

And then there was that smell that she knew so well. Paralyzed with panic, tears glistened in her eyes.

"Hello, my love," Jesse said.

She couldn't move. She said nothing.

"Aren't you going to greet me?"

She tried to speak, but only a broken syllable made it out of her mouth.

"You recognize the cologne, don't you?"

She didn't move. She didn't want to look at him.

"Don't you!" he shouted, causing her shoulders to jerk. "You always said if you smelled it again you'd know it was the man who attacked you. Well. Now you know. I saved it all these years. Didn't once consider throwing it away. I must have known on some level that we wouldn't last. But my. Six years. That's a very good run, don't you think?"

Harmony began to breathe through her mouth.

"Why don't you answer me?" Jesse asked, a bite in his tone.

"I can't." She swallowed.

"Turn around."

Harmony took a moment to close her eyes and squeezed her lips together. She told herself to gather some strength. Psychopaths loved to see people shake with fear.

"I said turn around."

Luckily she didn't need to wipe her face. The tears had welled but not fallen. Her eyes were dry enough to be seen now. She turned and faced him, clutching her hands together to keep them steady.

"Oh, Harmony, it's come to this."

He was smiling. She saw that he wasn't carrying a knife so he wasn't going to cut her, at least not yet.

"Are you ready to see Pete?"

"Is he alive?" She held her head high.

"Yes, he's alive. I wouldn't deprive you of seeing me slit his throat. Well, either that or sinking a knife into his heart. Can you imagine the geyser of blood that would bring? *Woo-ie*. What a sight to see. So I haven't decided. What do you think I should do?" He stepped closer and Harmony stepped back. That caused him to widen his smile, revealing his wolfish grin.

Harmony knew better than to try to reason with him. Psychopaths didn't care. He would just relish her desire to beat him, knowing she couldn't. Anything she said would be babble to his ears.

"Come on. Let's go in the house," Jesse said.

Harmony started to shake. She couldn't help it and it made him laugh. He had to love seeing her afraid. She knew it made him think he'd won a big prize. *Look how afraid I've made you? Look how scared you are? I did that.*

Jesse stepped even closer. Harmony was already against the VW and had nowhere to go. He reached out and did something she didn't expect. He slugged her in the jaw. Her neck snapped sideways, she fell and hit her head against the car's metal bumper. Harmony blacked out.

When Harmony came to, she was tied in a chair seated next to Pete, who remained unconscious. There was no gag in her mouth. Jesse either wanted her to be able to talk or thought it wouldn't matter if she screamed. No one could hear her.

Jesse grabbed her by the jaw and turned her head. "Would you look at that? You are going to have a shiner. I'm sorry about that, but I could see you were going to give me trouble."

"Why are you doing this? Explain it to me."

Jesse made a face of extreme bewilderment. "How can you call yourself a psychologist with a question like that? I ask you."

"You don't have to do this."

"Of course, I don't *have* to do this. I don't have to do anything! I want to do this. I relish this. You, my dear little bitch, had the gall to desire this mealy worm of a man . . . no, no, I can't even call him a man. You desire this mentally challenged, weak-minded fool over me?"

Harmony bit the side of her cheek, but she couldn't hold her tongue. "He wasn't always weak. He was getting better, still can get better. Whereas someone like you hasn't the option. Even with a lifetime of therapy, you'll always be a psychopath."

Her words did not illicit anger from Jesse. Instead, he sighed. "Ain't it the truth? I can't change. Although I did change for a while. Unintentionally, because of you. You do know that, don't you?"

"I don't know anything except Peter and I don't deserve this."

Jesse shrugged lackadaisically. He stepped over to the table, where Harmony saw an assortment of knives lined up side by side. He picked up a shiny one about seven inches long and admired it.

"What do you think of this knife?"

Harmony didn't say anything.

"Come on. You had a lot to say only a second ago."

"They'll all do the job, I suppose."

He eyed her. "They will. Well, except for this butter knife." He picked it up. "I was just joshing about that." He tossed it into the sink. "You know, trying to lighten things up a bit. Did it work?"

"Did I laugh?"

Jesse's affect went flat. "You're no fun." Still holding the deadly blade, he crossed to Pete and shook his knee. "I'm beginning to think I gave him too big a dose. He should have been awake by now. Pete. Pete. Wakey, wakey. Time to open your eyes."

Pete didn't stir. Jesse raised the knife and plunged the tip about an inch into Pete's thigh. Pete yelped.

"Leave him alone!" Harmony cried.

Jesse tossed a grin in her direction. Pete moved his head back and forth, eyes opening for only a second.

"Wake up, man!" Jesse stabbed him again with greater force. Pete cried out in pain.

"Stop it!" Harmony screamed.

Jesse chuckled.

Blood ran down Pete's pants leg and onto the floor. Jesse wrinkled his nose. "This is why we're in the kitchen. Easier clean-up." He looked at his hand holding the knife. Blood had spurted onto his skin. He grabbed a rag and wiped it.

Pete was awake now and his eyes were filled with fear.

"Got that adrenaline pumping, eh?" Jesse tossed the rag into the sink. "Yeah we did." He ruffled Pete's hair and looked over at Harmony. "Maybe you'd like a matching set? You know, the way people do with tattoos?"

"I have enough scars, courtesy of you," Harmony replied.

"You do, don't you? Maybe Pete." He looked at him. Pete's chin trembled.

"Peter. I'm so sorry," Harmony said.

"I'm so sorry, Peter," Jesse mimicked sarcastically. He looked down at his clothes. "I'm thinking I should change or kiss these threads goodbye. I have no idea how messy this will get. In the infamous words of Arnold, I'll be back."

Jesse left them alone.

Harmony tried to lean toward Pete, which was impossible. All she could do was crane her neck. "I can't believe this is happening."

He closed his eyes. A throb of his wounded thigh caused him to release a short moan. Then, surprisingly, he chuckled. "You did recommend him. Funny, that."

"It's not funny at all. I've known him for six years and I never suspected this was who he was." She jerked a couple of times in a useless effort to be free. "Our hands are tied with rope. I'd say let's try to scoot the chairs and untie ourselves but he'll be back any second. There isn't enough time."

Pete looked at the cutlery on the table and laughed. His eyes half-closed. His head lolled. "There're plenty of knives in here. Cutting the rope would be quicker. But we'd have to be fast."

"Lightning fast."

"Really, really lightning fast."

They both laughed. It was better than crying. But then tears began to trickle down Pete's cheek. "You know," he said softly. "There was a time when I wouldn't have cared if someone murdered me. You changed that."

Harmony closed her eyes. She'd helped him to care only to end up like this? "I would congratulate myself, but . . ."

"You gave me hope," Pete continued. "And given the situation we're in this may be the corniest thing I could say, but time has apparently run out for the two of us and . . ." He swallowed. "I love you. I do."

Harmony searched for the right words to reply. She thought of Pete's surprise visit to her in the backyard and wished she'd asked him to stay. She should have followed her heart and not the rules. People always claimed life was too short and she and Peter were about to prove them right. Now there was no time to explore their feelings, and they were in this situation because of her affection for him. Guilt consumed her. Tears flowed. It might be wrong, but she did love him. This was all her fault.

"Harmony?" Pete said. "Did you hear me? Do you have a response?"

Her voice was barely above a whisper. "I . . . I love . . ."

The tender moment of confession was destroyed when Jesse entered the kitchen. "Aw. Did I hear the L word being bandied around?" He put his face in Pete's and stared him in the eye. "You know, she says that a lot. She used to say it to me. The L word. I wouldn't put a lot of stock in it."

He poked the knife into Pete's neck, causing blood to trickle, but not a lot of damage. "You can call that a preview of coming attractions," Jesse sneered.

"You're horrible," Harmony said. "Sadistic and depraved."

Jesse chuckled and moved away, knife in hand. "I thought we could play a little game of truth-or-knife wound because I have a few questions for the two of you."

"Go fuck yourself," Pete said, showing Jesse some honest moxie for the first time.

Jesse threw the knife causing Harmony to scream. The weapon whizzed past Pete's ear and drove into the kitchen backsplash. "Would you look at that? I missed. Close. But that only counts in horseshoes and hand grenades."

He strolled to the table and picked out a second knife. "Let's see how this one does, shall we?" He moved into position and pretended to perfect his aim when the entire room erupted with the smell of gasoline. "What the hell?"

Pete and Harmony exchanged sideways glances. "My sister," Pete said.

"You think so?" Harmony answered, remembering the smell from her encounter with Andrea's ghost in the bathroom.

Pete nodded. "Without a doubt."

Jesse threw the knife out of anger. It went wide and high, tumbling into the wall and falling. "What are you two talking about?"

"My sister, if you really want to know," Pete responded. He groaned as the wound in his thigh throbbed again.

"It's not your sister. It's a gas leak," Jesse snarled.

"It's her signature scent," Pete responded.

"Shut up!" Jesse checked the oven again. He checked the gas dryer in the alcove off the kitchen. He left the room to inspect elsewhere.

"Why is she here?" Harmony asked.

"Call me crazy, but I think she wants to help us," Pete said.

The gas continued to drift through the house as Jesse returned.

"Maybe you should get out before the house blows," Harmony suggested.

"Maybe I should slit your throat here and now." He grabbed another knife and took several threatening steps toward her when suddenly the lights went out and Andrea's laugh permeated the room. Jesse stopped moving. It wasn't so dark it was impossible to see, but it was unsettling. The knife slipped from Jesse's fingers.

The kitchen door began to rattle. Someone was trying to get in. "Open up! This is the police. I have a warrant!"

"Thank God," Harmony said.

"Thank God, nothing. The cops are here, the gas leaked, and the lights went out. They did something." Jesse grabbed another knife and came for her, but an unseen force knocked his arm away. Then something shoved him backward. He lost the knife and lost his footing. He landed on his butt.

The knife levitated off the floor, moving away. He stared. His chest heaved with labored breath. "That can't be."

Andrea's laugh rang out and the knife was thrown with precision, slicing a piece of Jesse's cheek. He screamed in pain, blood gushing down his cheek, into his mouth, onto his shirt and the linoleum floor. Andrea's laugh grew maniacal.

The door continued to rattle, but the lock held. "Open the door!"

"No!" Andrea's shout echoed throughout the house.

"We have to try," Harmony told Pete. They began to scoot their chairs. Jesse staggered to the table and grabbed two knives. Just as something invisible shoved him back, he threw the knives in rapid-succession at Pete, then Harmony, then fell again.

One by one the knives rose from the table and one by one they shot at Jesse. He curled into a ball. "Stop!" he screamed. The knives landed point-perfect in the wood floor, encircling him. When no more came he snatched one, found his feet, and ran to the door. He had to be quick. The police continued to pound. The door rattled and shook. Jesse opened it. Detective Horton, about to use his shoulder as a battering ram, stumbled inside and fell. Jesse ran like a linebacker, shoving Guerrero aside as he swung the knife.

Three deputies aimed their pistols at Jesse, simultaneously shouting, "Freeze," but the guns went flying. Andrea's voice boomed: "He's mine."

The deputies scrambled for their weapons when they were hit with an awful smell.

"What's that?" asked one of the cops, wincing with revulsion.

"It's gasoline," Guerrero said.

"Where's it coming from?" a second cop asked.

"Who cares? We need to arrest him," the third deputy responded. Before he could take action, the odor intensified and he began to gag.

A light materialized thirty yards in front of them. Guerrero, along with the deputies, gawked in amazement.

"What the hell is that?" one deputy asked.

"How should I know?" another answered.

The light grew misty with a female form and a voice commanded, "Leave him. I told you. He's mine." The mist faded into nothing.

"I'm not going out there," a deputy said.

"Me either."

"I will," said the third.

"Don't be a hero," Guerrero told him. "We'll go together."

Jesse dashed like a rabbit on an adrenaline rush until he reached the rocks that camouflaged the entrance to his secret mine. Even then his momentum was so great that he slammed into the jagged edges, gouging his shoulder and scratching his face. He was in a world of hurt. His cheek stung and pulsed with pain. His muscles had been strained beyond their capacity and his mind was muggy, circling the twilight zone. What was real, what was not? What had gone wrong? He'd always been lucky, always gotten away with anything he wanted. Why were things different now?

Harmony. She'd destroyed him. He hated her.

His chest heaved in and out. He slid down the sharp, uneven rocks to the ground, hoping to catch his breath. It was dark now and his property was vast. For some reason they'd stopped coming for him and he'd gotten away. If he could slip inside the mine and stack rocks behind him to completely seal it off, they shouldn't find him.

He looked at his clothes. They were bloody and torn, courtesy of the jagged granite. *Good thing I changed.* He laughed at the ridiculous thought.

After a few minutes' rest, he slunk inside the mine and started to build a fortress, heaping all the rocks he could find. By the time he finished, he'd blocked the entrance, a foot thick. He was entombed. Enveloped in darkness, he used his hands to guide him along the granite face of the tunnel, slowly making his way toward the room with his beloved mementos. There he would find one of his lanterns.

Halfway to the room, he stopped. He didn't have a key to the wooden door. How would he ever get it open? He couldn't see. His eyes didn't adjust to the light because there was no light. He sank to the ground. Why bother? He'd wait his pursuers out. He could last a day or two before he knocked down the rocks he'd stacked to hide the entrance. Then he'd make a run for it. He'd leave California.

He put the knife on the ground, slid his knees up to his chest, and allowed his head to loll. He needed to rest. All the excitement had exhausted him. *I'm in my safe place*, he told himself, and closed his eyes, thinking he might sleep. It felt good to relax.

I'm safe.

But just as his breathing grew regular, he detected light though his closed eyelids.

That can't be right, he thought. *There is no light.*

"Jesse." His name floated through the air, syllables like a song, breathy but clear. He opened his eyes and a shockwave jolted his system. What was he looking at?

A woman wearing a sexy, clingy dress, with a long slit up the side, stood between him and the mine's rocked-in entrance. She seemed to glow. The gasoline odor surfaced once again. She took a step toward him, one shapely leg escaping through the slit. As she took a second step, the odor grew stronger.

Jesse's heart went into overdrive. He knew who this was. Double A. She was alive and had breached his mine.

I'm not alive and I've breached your mind. Her lips didn't move, but she spoke just the same.

He stood up, his eyes glued to the vision in front of him. Double A stopped walking. Her feet grew transparent and she appeared to float. He was mesmerized. She was beautiful, her face inviting, her eyes shining like glassy liquid opals. If this was a dream, he didn't mind. He wanted to touch her. He wanted to hold her. He wanted to feel her flesh, her skin, every curve.

What flesh? he heard her say.

He didn't understand, but that didn't matter. This was a dream and dreams were always spacey and disjointed.

What else? she asked with her still non-moving mouth.

"What else? What do you mean?" Jesse asked.

What else would you like to do to me?

"I'd like to kill you, of course."

She smiled and when she did, the skin of her face dripped like candle wax. The flesh fell away, too. The tissue that stayed turned to charcoal and Jesse smelled body tissue in the throes of fire. Her beauty transformed and she became a repugnant, grotesque, decaying corpse. Blood oozed from her nose and lifeless eyes. Maggots crawled in and out of her seared and blackened mouth.

Would you like to kiss me first? she asked.

A stench reached Jesse's nostrils. Double A was rotting before his eyes. He took a step backward and she floated forward. Dream be damned. This was too real.

I am real. Let me come closer and I'll show you.

Jesse shook his head. He continued to back up and she stayed with him until he decided it was time to run. He turned and sprinted into the blackness, sweat pouring from his brow, his lungs nearly bursting. He slammed into the locked trophy room door. If only he could go inside and be safe. But there was no safety. If she could get into the mine, she could get into the room. He looked over his shoulder. She was a mere five feet away, her glowing, socket eyes focused on him, her mouth shaped into a joyful, ruthless grin.

He turned and faced the blackness of the tunnel. Even with her illumination, he couldn't see what was in front of him. He began to run anyway. *Faster. Faster. I have to go faster.*

He could smell her rancid breath. He could feel it blow on the back of his neck.

Don't touch me. Don't touch me. My heart will rupture. I don't want to die.

He let out a scream and glanced over his shoulder again. She wasn't behind him. She was gone! He continued to move forward but slowed to a crawl. He stopped when he realized he was at the edge of the pit, one foot halfway over the side. God, if he'd continued he'd be a goner. Even if this was only a dream, he would probably have had a heart attack. As it was his heart was hammering at record speed. He placed a hand on his chest and took a step away from the drop.

"Calm down. Calm down. She's gone," he said.

No, I'm not. I'm right here.

He looked up. She hovered directly before him, her face maniacal, terrifying, and smelly. She hissed like a cobra. Jesse reacted with an involuntary step back and discovered he'd run out of ground. Teetering on the edge of the pit, his arms flew out from his sides and churned like circling windmill blades. But he couldn't gain his balance. After an eternity of seconds, he fell. His reverberating scream penetrated the air, cut to silence only when he hit the quarry below and joined the corpses he'd discarded.

Chapter 25

Peter and Harmony were surprised, yet pleased, when Esther invited them to her grandfather's retirement party. "It would mean a lot to him," she'd told them. They were the survivors of his final case. Living proof, so to speak, that what he did mattered. The two readily accepted.

The event was held at a popular Mexican restaurant on a Saturday. The place was packed. Clearly Detective Guerrero was well respected. Peter and Harmony learned that nearly everyone he ever worked with was there—even a Detective Berry, so said the event's host. The announcement caused many to laugh.

"Must be an inside joke," Harmony whispered to Peter.

The party began with a roast. Co-workers made fun of Guerrero's love of ginger chews, the color green he tended to wear, his Chevy that was a million years old, and even his coffee cup. No matter how many times he was gifted a new one with humorous "cop" references, he only used his World's Best Granddad mug.

"That coffee mug is years old. It's been broken and repaired," a fellow detective stated. "I hid it once and left one on his desk that said . . ." He grinned and laughed so hard he had to wipe a tear from his eye. "Well, never mind what it said. The point is, he knew I'd taken it. Spent an hour looking for it. And in the end threatened to arrest me for theft!"

The room erupted in laughter.

"He even took out his handcuffs and dangled them in front of me."

More laughter rippled through the room. Guerrero laughed, too. "I would have, too!" he called.

"I have no doubt," the detective replied. "Needless to say, I returned the mug and never touched it again."

The next "roaster" came to the podium with a smile and a shaking head. "After Donato became a widower," he began, "we respectfully waited a couple of years before some of us decided to play matchmaker."

Harmony glanced at the burly, retiring detective. His face said it all: *Shut up!* But the speaker remained clueless and continued on.

"Like the rest of us, our friend here enjoyed getting together for a drink after work, and we started asking—shall we say—some special guests to join us. After about three times, Donato caught on, but only because of . . ." He snapped his fingers as he tried to think. "Elaine. Yeah, Elaine. That was her name." He looked outward at the sea of faces until he saw a cop who looked like he could retire as well. "Wasn't she your sister-in-law, Owen?"

Owen nodded and rolled his eyes.

"Anyway," the speaker continued, "Elaine got a little tipsy and a little forward. Well, a lot forward. She must have liked what she saw because at some point she leaned in and planted a big fat one smack-dab on Donato's lips. I think he turned three shades of green."

Laughter once again filled the room.

"Blended right in with his shirt! After that he always seemed to come up missing when we asked around for who wanted to meet for a drink. We started to call him Gone Guerrero." The speaker raised a glass. "Well, now he'll be gone for a different reason. A great reason. Retirement, buddy. You earned it! Gone Guerrero, we'll miss you!"

Despite the sweet ending to the speech, Harmony thought Guerrero looked wounded.

The next speakers began to pay tribute to Guerrero's accomplishments. He had worked 265 homicide cases, some simple and some complex, and had an impressive 91% solve rate. He took his work to heart and hated to give up. Guerrero's boss pointed out that his career ended on a high note. His investigation of Archibald Bent's murder had led to the discovery of a serial killer and to that killer's grisly death. A tracking dog led police to the location of Jesse Evans' body in no time flat. It was poetic justice, Guerrero's boss said. The psychopath died in the very pit he'd used to dispose of his victims. The autopsy determined that Jesse had died of a massive heart attack, even though his heart appeared to be healthy. The coroner thought he'd died of fright. The look of utter terror cemented on his face seemed to confirm it.

Peter and Harmony gazed at each other. They knew the reason for Jesse's fear: Andrea. She had not only foiled Jesse's knife throws, she'd hunted down Jesse.

Jesse's story was big news, and Peter and Harmony had followed it. Excavation of the pit took several weeks. In the end, the authorities found sixteen corpses with Hawkeye, Katie Hammel, and Jordan Lyman the most recent. Clothing, IDs, and photos found in Jesse's trophy room, along with DNA testing, had determined the identities of some of the decomposed victims. The authorities hoped that in time all would be identified.

After the tributes, a ten-minute video Esther had put together played. It highlighted Guerrero's career and family. Images of Guerrero's wife, Sally, and the times they shared with their three daughters were touching. After the initial viewing, lunch was served and the video looped continuously in the background.

As the party wound down, people left. Guerrero sat alone at one of the round tables watching the video. Harmony and Peter approached to pay their respects, but slowed as they came closer. His shoulders were slumped as he gazed at the screen. A sense of melancholy emanated from him. They heard him murmur, "My love. My perfect love. I miss you." He took a shaky breath and looked away.

Esther appeared and took Harmony's arm. She spoke in a hushed tone. "My Grandmama, Mother, and aunties were t-boned by a drunk driver twelve years ago. He's lost his faith. The pain runs deep."

A tear trickled from Guerrero's eye. He'd heard his granddaughter and responded. "Dealing with death on a daily basis doesn't—didn't—help." He didn't look to see who Esther had spoken to.

"I've seen what human beings do to each other," Guerrero continued. "How can a loving God allow such things? Now I'm retired and except for Esther, my family is gone. It's time to hurry home. But to what? My empty house?"

"Detective Guerrero?" Harmony said.

He swiped his cheek. "Sorry," he said. It took a moment before he glanced up to see Harmony and Pete standing in front of him. His expression immediately brightened, then faded as his eyes traveled to the sling on Pete's right arm. He smiled when he caught sight of Pete's hand holding Harmony's.

Guerrero stood up and extended his hand. Pete shook it first, then Harmony.

"It's good to see you alive and well," Guerrero said. "What a scare that was. I understand the knife missed you completely, Dr. McKenna." He turned his eyes back to Pete's injured arm. "But you weren't so lucky."

"Pretty lucky. He missed my heart and lungs. The knife nicked an artery and I lost some blood. The chair fell over and I broke my arm. But the police were Johnny on the spot and the EMTs arrived in time. I'm on the mend."

"Good. Good." Guerrero's smile widened.

"Your investigation saved our lives," Harmony said. "And we wanted to thank you."

"Well, if I'd pushed a bit harder, you might not have gone through what you went through. I made some mistakes, I'm sorry to say."

"Be careful with those regrets. They can really mess you up. Take it from me," Pete said. "And my latest therapist."

"Ah!" Guerrero said. "I'll try to remember that."

"So. Retirement," Harmony said. "Big plans?"

"No plans, I'm sorry to . . ." He stopped himself. "It's a sobering thought to think your life's work is complete and that you have no one to, um . . . Well, my wife died several years ago, as Esther here just told you. I'm beginning to think this girl has no boundaries." He gave his granddaughter a frown.

"I have boundaries. But you've been mopey. Everyone can see. So I explained why. You miss your family and you put too much faith in worm food."

"When you're dead, you're dead," Guerrero said.

"Do you really believe that?" Pete asked. "After you and your entire law enforcement team saw my sister?"

Words caught in Guerrero's throat. He stared. "I don't know what we saw. Some sort of mass hysteria took place, I think. And how did you even hear about that?"

"I spent a couple days in the hospital. Andrea paid me a visit. She told me what she did."

A small amount of sarcasm crept into Guerrero's voice. "Did she explain why she set your nightclub on fire?"

"I always knew why she did that."

"Oh?" Guerrero said.

"Pure and simple jealousy. Although I guess I wouldn't say jealousy is ever pure or simple. It has such an impact on people if it isn't kept in check."

"And in your sister's case?"

"She'd just been released from prison and she wanted me to help her make a comeback. I had a lot of A-lister friends at the time. I'd written some number one hits. She wanted me to write a song for her which I'd already done. I was going to surprise her with it the night she started the fire. Unfortunately she got it into her head I was giving her the brush-off, and in a moment of madness, she did what she did. So, my big regret was not telling her up front that I'd written a song for her. If I had, none of those people would have died."

"Wow," Esther said, tightening her hold on her grandfather's arm. "Do Double A's fans have it wrong."

Harmony squeezed Pete's hand. "But he's letting go of the guilt now. He can talk about it. He's moving forward. He's even ready to work with his business partner to rebuild their club."

"Glad to hear it," Guerrero said.

"And," Harmony said. "He no longer feels a need to . . ."

Pete made a noise that stopped her mid-sentence.

"Feel a need to, what?" Guerrero asked.

Pete sighed. "Seek the help of Darius."

"Darius?" Guerrero questioned, surprised. "You know, we were able to obtain a court order to go through Jesse's files. It filled in a lot of the blanks about this case. One name in there we couldn't make heads or tails of was Darius."

"Darius," Harmony said. "He's . . ." Pete gave her a disapproving look. "He's very mysterious."

"He's a mystic," Pete explained. "He helped me."

Guerrero snorted.

"Maybe he could help you," Esther said.

Chapter 26

Detective Guerrero wasn't sure why he'd decided to take his granddaughter's advice and talk to Darius. Standing on the so-called mystic's doorstep, about to knock, he told himself he was sewing up loose ends. Darius might shed more light on Jesse.

The door opened quietly and a man with long, dark hair stood before him. He exhibited the most peaceful countenance Donato Guerrero had ever encountered. *"Namaste,"* the man said with a prayerful bow. "Would you like to enter?"

"Darius?" Guerrero said.

"Come in, by all means." Darius motioned with his hand.

The detective felt mesmerized. He followed Darius down the hall to a room filled with all the paraphernalia a mystic might put on display. Guerrero frowned, unconvinced by what he saw.

"Please. Sit down," Darius said. "The comfortable chair? Or the love seat?"

"The chair will do." Guerrero sat.

Darius presented him with a glass of water without even asking if he wanted one. The detective took it. His mouth was dry.

Darius sat and faced Guerrero. He didn't say anything. Instead, he smiled ever so slightly and gazed at Guerrero with clear, accepting eyes.

"My name is Donato Guerrero. I'm a . . . *was* a detective with the Los Angeles police department. I retired so I'm not here in any official capacity. I'm here because I want to satisfy my own curiosity about a few things. Mainly, about Jesse Evans."

Darius remained quiet and assured.

"What can you tell me about him?"

"Nothing you don't already know."

Guerrero sighed. He stood up and moved about, reading the inspirational messages on the walls. "What is it you do for a living?"

"I am me."

"You do 'me' for a living? I do 'me' but I earned money being a policeman."

"Ah. You want to know how I support myself. I help people."

"But you're not licensed for any of this." He made a circle in the air with his index finger.

"Do I need a license to help people?"

"Depends." Guerrero tried to strong-arm Darius with a stare. It didn't work. The detective looked away first.

It was Darius' turn to sigh. "You seem to suspect me of something nefarious."

"I'm sorry. It's the cop in me. Sometimes I can't turn it off."

"All right. I have a sense of you now. You want to know what I do. If you like, I will show you. But you have to trust me." Darius gazed placidly at the cop.

"Well, what are we talking about here?" Guerrero asked.

"A little guided meditation. A dive into your soul so that you reveal yourself to yourself."

Guerrero nearly cackled. "And I'll be cured?"

"I did not say that." He motioned at Guerrero with his hands. "But that's what you heard. See how it works?"

"The subconscious and all that."

"And all that. You must believe you need to be cured. Your term, not mine. I think 'released' is more fitting."

Guerrero was about to say "I'll pass" when he began to focus on Darius' hands. Their movement reminded him of a music conductor guiding his orchestra through the most melodious of tunes. He grew mesmerized. At times he could swear Darius' fingers merged with the air, becoming transparent then opaque again.

"Everyone needs to be released from something," Guerrero said. He stopped staring at Darius' hands. "Okay. Okay. I'll be your guinea pig."

"I will not be doing this for me."

"No. Uh. I want to do it."

"Then, please. Sit down again."

Guerrero sat in the chair. Darius put on some soft, peaceful, rhythmic music. "Close your eyes," he said. Guerrero did.

Darius told him to visualize a path meandering through a meadow. This path, he said, was a magical path and could take Guerrero anywhere: the sky, the mountains, a canyon, the past, the present, the future. His voice droned on until it seemed more like notes of music than words. Guerrero relaxed. He felt safe. He felt free. His imagination took over and he began to see many things.

He saw his family. His wife and all three of his daughters were enjoying Christmas Eve. Christmas songs played, the tree sparkled, towering over a mountain of presents. His wife Sally was in the kitchen making tamales with her sister. The kids were young and could only do as much as little ones could do when it came to homemade masa and corn husks. Time tilted and it was now midnight. Everyone was in the living room opening their gifts. Donato enjoyed a margarita as he watched the children squeal with delight.

The image shifted. The family was having a barbecue with neighbors. The kids were older, but still young, running around, loud and rambunctious. Donato was at the grill. His next door neighbor brought him a shot of tequila. About to drink it, he lost out to his wife when Sally walked up, snared the glass from his hand, and downed it herself. Everyone laughed.

The scene changed again. It was years later. The girls were in bed. Donato arrived home from work. Sally was livid. He was late. It was after one in the morning. Donato tried to explain that you don't pick your hours when you're a detective.

The scenarios came one after another. He walked his eldest daughter down the aisle and gave her away. His wife cried. She drank too much at the reception, grabbing anyone she could to dance, returning for another drink, dancing again, until she vomited on the reception room floor.

The next scene showed Donato and Sally living nearly separate lives. She slept in their bedroom. Donato fell asleep on the couch in front of the TV. When he awoke, he wandered off to a guest bedroom and tumbled into bed.

"I'm taking the girls and we're having a day of shopping. The four of us. Girls day out." The girls were grown. She should have said women's day out. Their eldest even had a five-year-old daughter and she'd finally managed to get pregnant again. Sally had been drinking. Donato could smell the alcohol. "Let Sofia drive!" he said, which only angered Sally. How much had she had, he wondered. "I mean it."

"Yeah, yeah. Sofia can drive."

He was at work when the call came. They were all dead. He'd lost them all. A drunk. A red light runner at sixty-five miles an hour had t-boned the car, knocking it into a power pole. Had Sally been driving? Yes. Did it matter? No. There were witnesses and cameras from businesses that recorded the entire thing. He never watched any of the footage. It would have broken him. Instead, he turned Sally into a saint who did no wrong.

"I'm not a saint," he heard Sally say. Her face was before him. Beautiful as it had always been, the age it was when she died. "Can you still love me if I'm not a saint?"

"You're a saint in my eyes," he replied.

"No. A woman with flaws. What you didn't see, I sideswiped a parked car just before this happened and didn't stop. I switched directions after that. I thought it would help me get away. If I hadn't switched . . . If I'd listened to our kids who told me to pull over, that drunk wouldn't have hit us."

Donato felt tears trickle down his cheeks.

"Can you forgive me?" Sally asked.

"I love you," he whispered. "Even with flaws."

The journey with his family vanished when he heard Darius speak. "I believe my work here is done."

Guerrero opened his eyes. He couldn't believe what he saw. The room was empty. There was no music, no posters, shelves, or furniture, and Darius was nowhere to be seen.

He left the apartment mystified. He knew he wasn't crazy, but he had no explanation for what had just occurred. As he stepped slowly down the stairs, a blond woman accosted him.

"What were you doing in there?" the woman demanded.

"That's a very good question," Donoto responded.

"Maybe I should call the police."

"I am the police. Or was." He slipped his identification from a pocket and held it up. "Retired as of a few days ago."

She exhaled with a frown. "You're still breaking and entering."

"I didn't break anything and Darius invited me in."

"Darius. Darius. Darius. Everyone mentions Darius. Who is Darius?"

"Another good question."

"The neighbor saw you go in and rang me. I was in the bath."

That was more information than he needed and he suppressed a smile. "I honestly can't explain what happened here. I'm as befuddled as you must be."

"I doubt that," she said. "There's something about this apartment."

She moved past Guerrero. He watched her put a key into the lock.

"It's been impossible to rent," she added. "The energy is too electric or something."

She opened the door and stuck her head in. "Strange. I don't feel it now." She looked at Guerrero. "What did you do?"

Guerrero laughed, but only for half a second. "Me? Honestly. Not a thing."

He continued down the stairs, shaking his head, wondering.

Epilogue

TEN YEARS LATER

Donato Guerrero pulled up to the curb in front of Peter and Harmony Ashton's estate in Beverly Hills. Peter had sold the big Bel Air mansion, and left it and its memories behind. The new house was much smaller, but still close to nine thousand square feet.

Donato took out his phone and let the Ashtons know he'd arrived. A security gate began to slowly open. Donato drove onto the property.

"It's good to see you," Peter said. "It's been two and a half years. That's too long."

After a hearty handshake, Donato sat on one end of the couch in the living room while Peter sat on the other. Harmony entered from the hall, carrying a teddy bear. "The boys are out like a light." As she noticed what she had in her hands, she chuckled. "Dylan is growing up. A month ago I couldn't have gotten him down for a nap without Buddy." She stuck out a lower lip to indicate a touch of sadness, and sank into the cushion next to her husband. He pulled her closer and kissed her cheek.

Harmony looked at the retired detective. "It's so good to see you, Donato. The last time you visited was when Sammy was born. Now, *he* does sleep with the blanket and the little lamb you brought him."

Donato smiled. "They grow fast. Esther is married. Well, you know that. You came to the wedding. She has three children now. I can hardly believe it. They're the apple of my eye," he said. "So much has changed. You know they tore down Archibald Bent's mansion? A developer built luxury condos."

"I didn't," Peter said.

"I drove by so I could see for myself," Donato said. "So now, somewhere in the new configuration, someone's living quarters takes up space where Archibald Bent was murdered." He shook his head.

"I wonder if the person who lives there ever feels the emotional impact of what happened." Peter looked downward. "Maybe he lays his head where Archibald's was lopped off."

"That's a morbid thought," Harmony said.

"Sorry." Peter squeezed her hand.

"Morbid or not, it's . . . We'll never know," Donato said. "It's sad. Nobody even remembers Archibald Bent now. On a lighter note, your nightclub is thriving?"

"I'm happy to say it is," Peter said. "Despite the calls for boycott early on by people who would have preferred a beautified empty lot with a sculpture and a plaque in memory of everyone who died. The new club is an unqualified success. People who are twenty-one now and coming to the club, were six when the first building burned down. They're too young to remember. All they want is a good time."

"Do people still say it's haunted?" Donato asked.

"Oh, those kinds of rumors crop up from time to time. They haven't caught on, probably because no one has actually seen anything. Now the Lucerne property is a different story."

"I heard," Donato said. "It's become a Mecca for ghost hunters. I even saw it featured on one of those ghost hunting shows. A medium claimed several spirits roam the property—the mine in particular."

"Jesse's victims," Harmony said.

"They used something called a spirit box and supposedly Hawkeye came through. The voice wasn't real clear. Now, when they asked questions with an electronic recorder, they caught the sound of a dog barking. We found a dog—Hawkeye's dog—in the pit. The recording gave me chills."

"It gives me chills to think Peter and I could have ended up in that pit," Harmony said.

"Thank God, you didn't," Donato said.

"Thank God?" Peter questioned. "You've changed your tune? Or was that just a figure of speech?"

"I plead the fifth." Donato laughed.

A middle-aged woman wearing a simple skirt and blouse entered the living room. "Lunch is ready," she said before turning away.

"Thank you, Janice," Harmony replied. "I thought we'd eat on the patio. Salad and toasted cheese sandwiches."

"Sounds great," Donato said. He pushed off the couch.

The table on the patio was set beautifully with a round, clear vase of orange roses in the center. Green salad was already in bowls at each place setting. Janice stood beside the table with a pitcher of iced tea in hand, ready to pour. One place had an eight by eleven piece of paper beside it, blank side up. Peter sat there.

"Do you ever think about Darius?" Peter asked pointedly, eyes on Donato.

The ex-cop snapped open a cloth napkin and placed it on his lap. Janice poured the iced tea.

"Thank you," Donato said.

"My pleasure," Janice replied.

Donato picked up a fork. "Funny question," he said. "Why do you ask?"

"Did you ever go see him?" Peter pressed.

Donato stifled a smile. "I did." He kept his eyes downward.

Harmony looked up from the bite of salad she was about to take. "You did?"

"Mm-hmm. The only person I ever discussed it with is Esther," Donato said. "Meeting Darius . . . Let's just say it gave me a sense of peace."

"Did you ever go a second time?" Harmony asked.

Donato looked at Harmony, then Peter. "I don't think there would have been any point to that."

"Why?" Harmony asked.

"He wouldn't have been there." Donato did not explain further. He still feared the experience meant he had gone a little bit crazy.

"I never felt the need to go back," Peter said. "Not after I got better. But I had dreams from time to time. Sort of like Darius was checking in on me."

Donato held his fork midair. "I had a dream like that. Only once. Very vivid."

Peter looked at Harmony and then Donato.

"What is it?" Donato asked.

"I came across something. A picture on the internet. Quite by accident," Peter said. "I wanted to show it to you." He turned over the piece of paper, revealing a black and white photo, and slid it toward Donato.

Donato put his glasses on. "What am I looking at?"

"It's a photo taken in 1969," Peter said.

Donato perused the photo. He saw a guru speaking to a number of people, all dressed in some version of the way Darius dressed. "Okay."

Peter leaned over and pointed out a man in the photo. "Who does that look like?"

Donato stared, then looked up with a start. "Darius."

"Plain as day," Peter said.

"It can't be if this was taken in 1969. That's over fifty years ago."

"I know," said Peter. "Then, right after I found this picture, I had a dream. Darius came to me and this time instead of just checking in, he gave me information. He told me that Jesse Evans was in hell. He's a soul filled with torment because he still feels no remorse for what he did. He did not tell me what hell was. Maybe it's feeling anguish. I don't know."

"I don't know either," Donato said.

"Andrea's soul is healing. She is still working on making amends. She feels all kinds of remorse. But she still has vengeful feelings and that's slowing her down. Jordan has reincarnated. Darius didn't say who he was. And Archibald is taking a break, resting so-to-speak, in between lives."

The two men looked at each other and said nothing. Harmony broke the tension. "The two of you are freaked out after all that happened because of a man who looks like Darius from 1969. Maybe it's Darius. Maybe it isn't. Maybe he really came to you in a dream. Maybe it's your subconscious still working things out."

The three looked at each other.

"I say, it's time to leave Jesse in the past," Harmony said.

The three of them began to eat.

**

After Donato left the Ashtons, he decided to go for a drive. He made his way to the apartment building in North Hollywood and parked across the street. It appeared a couple lived in Darius' old unit. He smiled as he watched two men climb the stairs, each carrying a bag of groceries. They unlocked the door and went inside. It was the ultimate proof that Darius had completed his mission in NoHo and moved on.

"If Darius can move on . . . ," Donato whispered.

He put the car in gear. He decided that when he got home he was going to ask to see his grandkids that night. He was going to play with them and enjoy every moment, because even though, apparently, souls continued on, life as a human on Earth was short and Donato intended to enjoy every second that he could.

AUTHOR NOTES AND ACKNOWLEDGEMENTS

Author Michael Raff and I venture forth as Nevermore Enterprises to meet the public and sell our books at horror conventions. For years he's been telling me *Chapel Playhouse* and *The Accordo* are horror novels. I would push back and say they were paranormal mysteries. Well, they are paranormal mysteries, but they are also horror novels. After the light bulb lit up in my head, I knew I shouldn't have been so stubborn. I also knew I needed to write another novel that fit the horror genre from the get-go.

I had a great deal of fun writing *The Haunting of Peter Ashton* and would like to thank those who helped me bring it to fruition. Thank you to my critique group colleagues, Freddi Gold and Michael Raff, for their critical eye. Thank you to author Holly La Pat (aka Sierra Donovan) who read the completed early drafts of this novel and made important suggestions and corrections. I was able to move forward more rapidly and confidently because of her. Also, thank you to my sister Helen O'Brien who read the completed manuscript and provided valuable insights. Thank you, as well, to Jenny Margotta, for quickly making the cover of this book and revising anything I asked for without complaint.

Finally, thank you to my husband Chuck for always encouraging me. He truly is my best friend and love.

Made in the USA
Columbia, SC
06 July 2024